W9-AAP-781

Rumpole Misbehaves

A NOVEL

JOHN MORTIMER

PENGUIN BOOKS

PENGUIN BOOKS
Published by the Penguin Group
Penguin Group (USA) Inc., 375 Hudson Street, New York, New York 10014, U.S.A.
Penguin Group (Canada), 90 Eglinton Avenue East, Suite 700, Toronto,
Ontario, Canada M4P 2Y3 (a division of Pearson Penguin Canada Inc.)
Penguin Books Ltd, 80 Strand, London WC2R 0RL, England
Penguin Ireland, 25 St Stephen's Green, Dublin 2, Ireland (a division of Penguin Books Ltd)
Penguin Group (Australia), 250 Camberwell Road, Camberwell,
Victoria 3124, Australia (a division of Pearson Australia Group Pty Ltd)
Penguin Books India Pvt Ltd, 11 Community Centre, Panchsheel Park, New Delhi – 110 017, India
Penguin Group (NZ), 67 Apollo Drive, Rosedale, North Shore 0632,
New Zealand (a division of Pearson New Zealand Ltd)
Penguin Books (South Africa) (Pty) Ltd, 24 Sturdee Avenue,
Rosebank, Johannesburg 2196, South Africa

Penguin Books Ltd, Registered Offices:
80 Strand, London WC2R 0RL, England

First published in Great Britain as *The Anti-Social Behaviour
of Horace Rumpole* by Penguin Books Ltd 2007
First published in the United States of America by Viking Penguin,
a member of Penguin Group (USA) Inc. 2007
Published in Penguin Books (UK) 2008
Published in Penguin Books (USA) 2008

1   3   5   7   9   10   8   6   4   2

Copyright © Advanpress Ltd., 2007
All rights reserved

PUBLISHER'S NOTE
This is a work of fiction. Names, characters, places, and incidents are either the product
of the author's imagination or are used fictitiously, and any resemblance to actual persons,
living or dead, business establishments, events, or locales is entirely coincidental.

THE LIBRARY OF CONGRESS HAS CATALOGED THE HARDCOVER EDITION AS FOLLOWS:
Mortimer, John Clifford, 1923–
Rumpole misbehaves : a novel / John Mortimer.
p.   cm.
ISBN 978-0-670-01830-7 (hc.)
ISBN 978-0-14-311411-6 (pbk.)
1. Rumpole, Horace (Fictitious character)—Fiction.   I. Title.
PR6025.O7552R795 2007
823'.914—dc22   2007037323

Printed in the United States of America

Except in the United States of America, this book is sold subject to the condition that it shall not, by
way of trade or otherwise, be lent, resold, hired out, or otherwise circulated without the publisher's
prior consent in any form of binding or cover other than that in which it is published and without
a similar condition including this condition being imposed on the subsequent purchaser.

The scanning, uploading and distribution of this book via the Internet or via any other means
without the permission of the publisher is illegal and punishable by law. Please purchase only
authorized electronic editions, and do not participate in or encourage electronic piracy
of copyrighted materials. Your support of the author's rights is appreciated.

For Ross

'. . . the Social Contract is nothing more or less than a vast conspiracy of human beings to lie to and humbug themselves and one another for the general Good.'

H. G. Wells, *Love and Mr Lewisham*

'. . . the statutory provisions relating to anti-social behaviour orders (ASBOs) are not entirely straightforward . . .'

Anti-social Behaviour Orders: A Guide for the Judiciary

I

The life of an Old Bailey hack has more ups and
downs in it than the roller-coaster on the end of
Brighton Pier. At one moment you may be starring
in a sensational murder in Court Number One at
the Ludgate Circus Palais de Justice, and the next
you're down the Snaresbrook Magistrates' on a
trivial matter of purloining a postal order or the
receiving of stolen fish.

I was smoking a small cigar in my room in
Chambers, contemplating the uncertainties of the
legal life, and comforting myself with the thought

that when you're on a down the up can't be far away, when there entered Soapy Sam Ballard, QC (the letters in my book stood for Queer Customer), our so-called Head of Chambers in Equity Court.

'You weren't at the Chambers meeting, Rumpole?' Soapy Sam uttered the words in the solemn tones of a judge in a case of multiple rape preparing to pass sentence.

'No,' I told him. 'I stayed away. When it comes to vital matters such as the amount of the coffee money or the regrettable condition in which some of our members leave the downstairs loo, I know I can trust you to deal with them with your usual panache.'

These words were kindly meant, but Soapy Sam continued to look displeased, even censorious. 'You missed a very important occasion, Rumpole. We were discussing the most serious problem that faces us all today.'

'You mean the fall in the crime rate, which has left me particularly short of briefs, or the elevation of the Mad Bull, now Mr Injustice Bullingham, to the High Court Bench?'

'Nothing like that, Rumpole. Something far more serious.'

'What could be more serious?'

'Global warming.' Soapy Sam uttered the words with almost religious solemnity.

'Really? On my way to Chambers this morning I noticed a distinct nip in the air.' It was a damp and windy March.

'The North Pole is melting, Rumpole. The seas are rising all over the world. The Thames will probably overflow the Embankment and there is a real possibility of the ground-floor rooms in our chambers being submerged. And you occupy a downstairs room, Rumpole.' He added the final sentence with, I thought, a sort of morbid glee.

'What am I expected to do about it?' I felt I had to ask. 'Stand in the Temple car park and order the tide to turn back? My name's not Canute, you know.'

'We know exactly what your name is, Rumpole.' Sam Ballard was giving me one of his least pleasant looks. 'And we have identified you as a source of pollution.'

'Well,' I said, adopting the reply sarcastic, 'that's nice of you.'

'You pollute the atmosphere, Rumpole, with those dreadful little brown things you smoke.'

'Cigarillos,' I told him. 'Available from the tobacconist just outside the Temple gate. Can I offer you one?'

'No, Rumpole, you certainly cannot. And I would ask you to consider your position with regard to the environment very carefully. That is all I have to say. For the moment.'

With that, our Head of Chambers gave a final sniff to the atmosphere surrounding me and then withdrew, closing the door carefully behind him. In a moment of exaggerated concern, I wondered if he was chalking a fatal cross on the other side of my door to warn visitors and prospective clients of the source of plague and pollution to be found within.

Dismissing such thoughts, I lit another small cigar and wondered if, as I struck the match, I could hear the distant sound of an iceberg melting, or at least the Thames lapping at the door. All was quiet, however. But then the telephone rang with news that put the environment firmly back into second place among my immediate concerns.

'There you are, Bonny Bernard, and it's good to hear from you,' I said, giving my favourite and most faithful solicitor a polite welcome. 'What are you bringing me? A sensational murder?'

'I'm afraid not, Mr Rumpole. Not this week.'

'An armed robbery at the Bank of New South Wales?'

'Not that either.'

'Don't tell me.' I'm afraid my voice betrayed my disappointment. 'Not another gross indecency in a picture palace?' Wartime epics were, I had found, the most likely to produce such regrettable behaviour in the auditorium.

'No, Mr Rumpole. None of those, I'm afraid. It's just that one of the Timson family wishes to retain your services.'

This was encouraging. The Timsons, an extended south London family whose members were seldom out of trouble, could usually be relied upon to keep She Who Must Be Obeyed in such luxuries as Vim, Mansion Polish, saucepan scourers, potatoes and joints of beef, as well as ensuring that I was provided with the necessities of life, such as the odd case of Château Thames Embankment from Pommeroy's Wine Bar.

'Which Timson are we talking about exactly?'

'Bertie, he says his name is.'

'Bertie Timson? I am trying to remember. Was it a case of carrying house-breaking, or even bank-breaking, implements? Did I get him off?'

'You did,' Bernard assured me. 'And he remembers you with gratitude. That's why he wants you to look after his boy, Peter.'

'Has Peter murdered someone?'

'Hardly. He's only twelve years old. Bertie re-married a bit late in life.'

'Well, for God's sake, what was young Peter's crime?'

'Football.'

'Is football a crime nowadays?' In a way I was glad to think so, remembering miserable days on a wet playing field at school, half-heartedly pressur-ing a soggy ball through mud.

'It is if you play it in the wrong sort of street. Peter's been served with an ASBO. He's due to come up before the magistrates. Bertie Timson's afraid his boy might go inside if he reoffends. That's why he wants to retain your services.'

'Is there any ready money in this retainer?'

'We can't expect that, not for defending a twelve-year-old.'

'I thought as much.'

'But you will consider yourself retained?'

'I suppose so.'

It had come to that. The advocate whose sen-sational career started when he won the Penge Bungalow Murders, alone and without a leader, was reduced to a retainer in the case of an anti-social behaviour order on a child. Of course, I never guessed at that time what strange results young Peter's illicit football would lead to. If I had, I would have accepted his father's retainer with more enthusiasm.

2

Extract from the Memoirs of Hilda Rumpole

Rumpole is down in the dumps. He is suffering from an acute shortage of work, which makes him almost impossible to live with. Rumpole in a high mood, when he's engaged in an important murder trial, for instance, is not an easy man to live with either. If he wins such cases it's even more embarrassing, and I'm expected to listen to quotations from his final speech and asked if I had ever heard of a better courtroom advocate. When he is down in the dumps, however, and without any interesting briefs, he tends to sit in silence, only occasionally asking if we couldn't cut down on such essentials as household cleaning materials.

As I have recorded in previous chapters of these memoirs, I met Sir Leonard Bullingham, now a High Court judge, at bridge afternoons in the house of my friend Marcia Hopnew, known as Mash. Leonard (this was before he got elevated and was merely Judge Bullingham at the Old Bailey) took, as you may remember, a considerable shine to me, and went to the lengths of proposing that I should divorce Rumpole and marry him. I found this proposition unacceptable when he suggested that we should take dancing lessons and go to tea dances at the Waldorf Hotel. I didn't fancy myself doing the tango among the teacups, thank you very much, so I turned Leonard down.

All the same, we kept meeting and playing bridge whenever the newly appointed Sir Leonard had a free afternoon. I always enjoy the post-mortem discussions after each round.

'If you'd led a small Spade,' I told Leonard after our game was over, 'we could have finessed their Queen. As it was, you led a Heart for no particular reason that I could see.'

'Wonderful!' Leonard looked at me with admiration.

'It wasn't wonderful at all. You should have remembered that I'd bid Spades.'

'No, it's wonderful that you have such an incisive mind, Hilda. And a clear memory for every card that's played. These are the sort of talents needed for a great courtroom advocate. Pity you never considered reading for the Bar.'

Well! I didn't say any more at the time, but the thought was planted. If my mind was so incisive, why shouldn't I make a better hand at being a barrister than Rumpole, who apparently has no work in view except a small boy's footballing offences?

After we had settled the scores, and worked out that he and I had won two pounds fifty pence, the High Court judge said, 'I know you've elected to stand by Rumpole through thick and thin, Hilda. But I hope that doesn't prevent us having another occasional date. Purely platonic, of course.'

I told Leonard that I would have no objection to meeting him occasionally. I didn't care for that 'platonic' thing he mentioned. As though he flattered himself that there was a chance of it being anything else.

The truth was that I needed Leonard's help in what has now become my Great Decision. I will read for the Bar!

3

AS A RESULT OF THE RECENT
CHAMBERS MEETING, 4 EQUITY
COURT HAS BEEN DECLARED
A NON-SMOKING AREA.
SMOKING WILL NOT BE PERMITTED
IN ANY PART OF THE BUILDING,
INCLUDING THE UPPER AND
LOWER TOILETS. IN FUTURE
ONLY NON-SMOKERS WILL BE
ADMITTED TO PUPILLAGE.
COFFEE WILL STILL BE PROVIDED AT

A REASONABLE COST, BUT THE
CONSUMPTION OF BEERS, WINES, SPIRITS
AND FOOD ON THE PREMISES
IS STRICTLY FORBIDDEN.

SIGNED: Samuel Ballard, QC

Now, at that time in the Rumpole history, when crime and therefore briefs appeared to be a bit thin on the ground, I had given up the luxury of a pie and pint of Guinness in the pub and instead had to put up with sandwiches for lunch. What with the search of our bags for terrorist devices, I had to smuggle in these sandwiches in the folds of the Rumpole mac. I went, on a dull morning out of court, to Pommeroy's for a bottle of their very cheap and ordinary to wash down my lunch. It was while I was enjoying this picnic that Luci Gribble, our newly appointed Director of Marketing and Administration, came into my room and sat down, looking at me with a sort of amused despair.

'You're a hopeless case, Rumpole,' she said.

'Am I really? I rather like hopeless cases. They're the ones I usually manage to win.'

'Well, I don't think you're going to win this time.

Haven't you seen the notice put up by our Head of Chambers?'

'I have, and I read it with interest.'

'You seem to be breaking every one of the new rules in Chambers, eating, drinking and smoking a small cigar.'

'Of course, Soapy Sam's notice clearly doesn't apply to me.'

'Why not? You're a member of Chambers.'

'But I didn't attend the Chambers meeting.'

'You never attend the Chambers meetings.'

'Exactly! So the decisions they come to are only binding on those who attend. They are *res inter alios acta.*'

'What's that meant to mean?' It was clear that Luci had even less Latin than I had.

'A thing decided among others. Leaving me free to do as I please.'

'I don't think that's much of a defence.' Luci looked sceptical. 'I mean, you weren't present when they passed the laws against murder, but that doesn't mean you can go about killing people.'

I suppose our Director of Marketing had a point there, but I found her next remark quite ridiculous. 'Erskine-Brown is considering the possibility of getting an ASBO against you, Rumpole.'

'An anti-social behaviour order?'

'That's the one.'

'Against me, did you say?'

'Exactly.'

'And what's the nature of their complaint?'

'Persistent smoking in Chambers, and bringing food and alcoholic refreshments into your room.'

'That's not anti-social behaviour. It's entirely social. Sit down, my dear old Director of Marketing. Let me offer you an egg sandwich, prepared by the hand of She Who Must Be Obeyed. Bring a spare glass and I can offer you a cheap and cheery mouthful. Now what could be more social than that?'

'Don't be ridiculous, Rumpole.'

'What's ridiculous about it?'

'If I accepted your hospitality . . .'

'Yes?'

'Then I'd be as anti-social as you are.'

At this our Director of Marketing left me feeling profoundly anti-social so far as Ballard and his devious sidekick, Claude Erskine-Brown, were concerned.

There is a certain area of London, not far from Clapham Common, where the streets of the wealthier middle classes, such as Beechwood Grove, are perilously close to less respectable areas, such as Rampton Road, which have become inhabited by members of the ever-spreading Timson clan, among them Bertie Timson, his wife, Leonie, and their single child, the twelve-year-old Peter. Bertie Timson's alleged trade as an 'Electrical Consultant' was in fact a cover story for more felonious trans-actions, but he was a polite enough client, and I remember him thanking me warmly after a success-ful defence on a charge of carrying house-breaking implements. He had done his time during Peter's extreme youth and now, when his son got into trouble, he had remembered Rumpole.

Peter and his friends frequently engaged in foot-ball games in Rampton Road which the neighbours apparently suffered without protest. However, on too many occasions the ball found its way into the quiet and respectable precincts of Beechwood Grove. After a number of complaints, the police were called. When Peter Timson pursued a flying ball into Beechwood Grove, he alone was appre-hended, as the rest of the team scarpered. Appar-ently Peter was considered to be the ringleader and source of all the trouble.

*

So I walked one Monday morning, with rain dribbling down from a grey sky, into the South London Magistrates' Court to defend a serious case of wrongfully kicked football. Madam Chair, hawk-nosed and sharp-eyed, with a hair-do which looked as though it had been carved out of yellow soap, sat between two unremarkable bookends, a stout and pink-faced man with a Trade Union badge in his lapel and a lean and hungry-looking fellow who might have been a schoolmaster.

'It's unusual for the defendant to be represented at this stage of the ASBO proceedings, Mr Rumpole. We wonder that you can spare the time from your busy practice.' Madam Chair sounded coldly amused.

'Then wonder on,' I told her, 'till truth make all things plain. Busy as I am, and I am of course extremely busy, I can always spare time for a case in which the liberty of the subject is an issue.'

'Your young client's liberty won't become an issue unless he breaks an anti-social behaviour order. We are all concerned with the liberty of the subject to enjoy peace from noisy footballers. Mr Parkes, I'm sure that you have a statement.'

The person addressed as Parkes appeared to be some eager young dogsbody from the local council.

He handed a document up to the bench and began to read the statement of a Mrs Harriet Englefield of 15 Beechwood Grove. She said she was a 'healer' by profession and had many clients whom she was able to treat for physical and nervous disorders in a peaceful and homely atmosphere. She also had an aged mother who had been ordered long periods of rest and tranquillity, which had become impossible owing to the noisy games of football played by 'rough children who come pouring in from Rampton Road'.

It was at this point that I rose to object. 'No doubt this Mrs Harriet Englefield will be giving evidence on oath?'

'The law has advanced a little since your call to the Bar, Mr Rumpole. We don't need to trouble such witnesses as Mrs Englefield. We are entitled to proceed on her written statement,' Madam Chair told me.

'So you are prepared to decide a criminal matter on hearsay evidence?'

'It's not a criminal matter yet, Mr Rumpole. And it won't be unless your client breaks the order we've been asked to make.'

'And plays football again?'

'Exactly!'

'Very well. I take it that even if we have dispensed with the rule against hearsay evidence, I am still allowed to address the court?'

This request was apparently so unusual that Madam Chair had to seek advice from the clerk of the court, who stood up from his seat below her throne to whisper. This advice she passed on in a brief mutter to her bookends. Then she spoke.

'We are prepared to hear you, Mr Rumpole, but make it brief.'

'I shall be brief. What is anti-social behaviour? If you ask me, I would say that the world has advanced towards civilization by reason of anti-social behaviour. The suffragettes behaved anti-socially and achieved the vote. Nelson Mandela's anti-social campaign brought justice to South Africa. Now this young person, this child I represent . . .'

I turned to wave a hand towards the long-haired twelve-year-old with curiously thoughtful brown eyes. 'This young Peter, or Pete, Timson.'

'Who is neither a suffragette nor Nelson Mandela,' Madam Chair thought it fit to remind me.

'That is true,' I had to admit. 'But he is an

innocent child. He has no criminal record. He has broken no law. If football is illegal, it should be forbidden by an act of Parliament. Don't stain his blameless record by a verdict based on untested hearsay evidence.'

'Is that all, Mr Rumpole?' Madam Chair broke into my final dramatic pause.

'All,' I said. 'And more than enough, in my submission, to let this child go back to playing.' With this I sat down, in the vain hope that I might have touched, somewhere in Madam Chair, a mother's heart.

After further whispered conversations the Chair spoke. 'Mr Rumpole's speeches,' she said, 'may be thought amusing in the Central Criminal Court, but here we cannot let his so-called oratory distract us from our clear duty. Peter Timson.' Here, prompted by an usher, my client rose to his diminutive height. 'We make an order forbidding you to enter Beechwood Grove for any purpose whatsoever, including, of course, the playing of football.'

When I went to say goodbye to my client, he was standing next to his father, Bertie.

'Say thank you to Mr Rumpole. I suppose he did his best.'

'Thank you, Mr Rumpole.' Peter seemed extraordinarily pleased with the result. 'I got an ASBO! All them down Rampton Road are going to be *so* jealous.'

I had never, in all my legal life, met so delighted a loser.

Back in Chambers I poured out the last glass from a bottle of Château Thames Embankment and lit a small cigar. My spirits were at a low ebb. My practice seemed to have shrunk to Pete-sized proportions. Then, quite unexpectedly, the tide turned. The telephone rang and I picked it up to hear once again the voice of my favourite solicitor.

'I'm sorry about the ASBO case,' Bonny Bernard said. 'But I think I might soon be in a position to offer you a murder.'

4

The case Bonny Bernard had sent me seemed in the best tradition of English murders since the far-off days of Jack the Ripper and the Camden Town affair. The tragedy of the unfortunate girls who go on the game is that they all too easily fall victim to manual strangulation.

The difference between these classic cases and the brief I was eagerly noting was that, in my present case, a death in Flyte Street, a small turning off Sussex Gardens near to Paddington Station, the alleged culprit was arrested in the dead girl's room and there seemed to be no mystery about it.

My client was Graham Wetherby, thirty-three, single, a clerk in a government department. He had an address in Morden, on the outskirts of London, and, according to his statement, he lived alone in a bed-sitting room, travelling up every day to Queen Anne's Gate and the Home Office.

The case against Wetherby was a simple one. On the date in question he telephoned the address in Flyte Street where Ludmilla Ravenskaya, a Russian immigrant, carried on her profession. His call was answered by Anna McKinnan, who acted as Miss Ravenskaya's maid and was the main witness for the prosecution. My client left his work at lunchtime and just before one he was admitted to the house in Flyte Street for a brief, expensive and, as things turned out, totally disastrous tryst.

The entry phone at the front door invited him up to a room on the second floor. Once there he dealt with Anna McKinnan, the maid, and paid over to her the £110 he had saved up for a brief moment of passion.

From then on McKinnan's evidence was clear. She told Graham Wetherby that he could go into the small sitting room and wait, and Ludmilla, the 'young lady', would come out to him. If she didn't come in a reasonable time he could knock on the bedroom door to announce his presence, because her mistress was alone and had no one else in with her. Accordingly, he went into the sitting room. Some twenty minutes later, McKinnan heard her 'young lady' screaming. She hurried into the sitting room and described what she saw.

The bedroom door was open and Wetherby was standing by the bed, on which the 'young lady' lay partially dressed. She could see red marks round her neck and she was lying across the bed in an attitude the maid called 'unnaturally still'.

Wetherby said nothing, but Anna McKinnan, according to her evidence, acted quickly. She went and locked the sitting-room door, making my client a prisoner. While he was shouting and hammering at the door, she telephoned the police from a phone in the kitchen.

A detective inspector, a woman officer and a police doctor arrived at the flat surprisingly quickly, no more than an hour later. McKinnan was able to tell them that she had seen Ludmilla alive and laughing over a cup of tea after her previous customer had departed.

She then let the officers into the sitting room, where a distracted Graham Wetherby told them he had found Ludmilla dead when, having knocked on the door and got no reply, he went into the bedroom.

On the face of it this seemed an unanswerable case, but I hoped that, when I got the chance of talking to Wetherby, some sort of defence might emerge. My pessimism was increased, however, the following morning, when I rang Bonny Bernard to thank him for the brief.

'I thought you'd like to know,' the misguided solicitor told me, 'that I've briefed a leader for you, your Head of Chambers, Mr Samuel Ballard, QC. It's a terrible business, isn't it?'

'Absolutely ghastly,' I agreed, deliberately mis-understanding his point, 'getting Soapy Sam Ballard to lead me. After all we've gone through together. How could you do it?'

'The client wanted a QC. He said in all the big murder trials they have QCs.'

'So you suggested Soapy Sam?'

'He's your Head of Chambers.'

'So you're determined to lose this case?'

'Is it – entirely hopeless?'

'No case is entirely hopeless unless you bring Mr Ballard in to conduct it.'

There was a silence, then Bernard said, 'I'm sorry.

The client insisted on Queen's Counsel. You're not Queen's Counsel, are you, Mr Rumpole?'

'Not yet,' I warned him. 'But who knows what may happen in the fullness of time?'

'Who knows? You're right there, Mr Rumpole.' My solicitor sounded encouraging. 'Meanwhile, I'll meet you and Mr Ballard in Brixton Prison. Looking forward to it.'

But I was no longer looking forward to our first meeting with our client, an occasion on which I would occupy a secondary and subordinate position. If, by any chance, there was some sort of defence available to Graham Wetherby, my not particularly learned leader could be guaranteed to miss it.

5

Extract from the Memoirs of Hilda Rumpole

Leonard has been helping me in the plan I have
for learning the law. He has lent me a number of
little books that he said he used for passing his
exams, his 'little crammers' he calls them. There's
one called *All You Need to Know about Contracts* and
another, which I found far more readable, called
Murder and Offences against the Person in a Nutshell.

Leonard Bullingham tells me I'll soon get to
know as much law as Rumpole. In fact, he doesn't

think that Rumpole knows much law at all and that the only thing he has going for him is his 'gift of the gab'.

He, Rumpole I mean, came home the other night in a high mood. I don't know which is more irritating, when he's in a high mood or down in the dumps. Anyway, he brought another bottle of wine home and announced that he'd be back in Court Number One at the Old Bailey. Mr Bernard had brought him some unsavoury case about a prostitute strangled in a flat near Paddington Station. It was while he was pouring out yet another glass of the wine from that dreadful little bar, and telling me more than I cared to know about the effects of manual strangulation, that I brought him up short by saying, 'It's a pity that someone has to die to really cheer you up, Rumpole.'

I'd silenced him for a while, and then he said, 'That's a terrible thought. Ludmilla from Russia, yes, of course. She's dead and no one can do anything about that. But there's that young man in Brixton Prison, that Graham Wetherby, he's not dead and is probably in need of a little help.'

'Why?' I asked. 'Why help him? He killed her.'

'We don't know that. And we shan't know it until twelve honest citizens come back into court and tell us so. Meanwhile,' and here Rumpole gave me one of those secret smiles of his that can be so annoying, 'there are one or two small points that might be of interest. We shall have to wait and see.'

So Rumpole went to bed in a comparatively happy mood, but the next day he was down in the dumps again because he'd been given a leader and wouldn't be able to do all of that unsavoury murder case he is engaged on at the moment. Speaking for myself, I have always found Samuel Ballard a most agreeable person who has given me a warm welcome at Chambers parties and who seems to understand some of the difficulties which arise from the fact of being married to Rumpole.

'He'll be able to take over the case and lose it,' Rumpole said. 'Losing cases is what he has a real talent for. And it's just because he's entitled to write QC after his name.'

'It's a pity you can't write QC after *your* name, Rumpole,' I told him. 'Then you wouldn't have to rely on Ballard.'

'I don't rely on Ballard.' Rumpole was not taking this well. 'I just have to make sure he relies on me.'

'But you're the number two, Rumpole. I really don't know why you can't get to write QC after *your* name. You've been there at the Bar long enough.'

'My face doesn't fit.' Rumpole shook his head, I thought a little sadly.

I took a long and critical look at his face. At least I could truthfully say, 'Lots of people with worse faces than yours have been able to put QC after their names.'

'I mean, judges tend not to like me. You have to get judges on your side to get made a Queer Customer. They don't like the way I point out their mistakes. They don't appreciate it when I get juries to notice their devious methods of trying to secure a conviction. They can tell that when I say, "In my humble submission to Your Lordship", I can't bring myself to feel humble at all.'

'Perhaps you should stop doing those things, Rumpole,' I suggested. 'It's so embarrassing to have to admit to our bridge club that you're still a *junior* barrister. At your age too!'

'I can't stop being myself,' he told me. 'That's too much to ask. All the same, I might try it. I might apply for a silk gown and a seat in the front row. Horace Rumpole, QC. It has an agreeable ring to it!'

The next time I played bridge with Mr Justice Bullingham, I told him that Rumpole was seriously thinking of applying for silk.

'Good for him,' Sir Leonard said, I thought generously. 'But I'm afraid he won't get it.'

'Why ever not?'

'The trouble with Rumpole is, and this is the generally held opinion, his face doesn't fit.'

6

'There was a notice in a telephone box near where I went for lunch. "Exotic young Russian lady gives a full personal service".'

'And what did you take that to mean?' Soapy Sam, unfortunately my leader, asked the question in the Brixton interview room.

'Well, it didn't mean shoe cleaning,' I might have told him, 'or even an extra shampoo and scalp massage.' But I tactfully held my tongue.

Our client answered the question. 'I thought it meant we could make love,' he said. And I thought that word 'love' sounded strange, even shocking, in those surroundings.

Graham Wetherby, who had uttered it, seemed an ordinary, polite, inoffensive young man. His face might have looked pleasant enough had it not been disfigured by a red birthmark which stretched from under his eye about halfway down his left cheek.

'We don't all have convenient and loving home lives, Mr Ballard. Some of us have to venture a bit further afield.'

He had an oddly precise way of speaking, with his lips pouted. I remember a saying of my childhood: 'Prunes and prisms, very good words for the lips.' Graham Wetherby seemed to have learned to speak in the 'prunes and prisms' way.

'The absence of a love life,' Ballard now put on a look of severe displeasure, 'doesn't mean you have to visit premises such as 16 Flyte Street.'

'No, sir. Of course not. I do realize that. In my saner moments.'

'Are you telling us you are insane when you do these terrible things?' Ballard asked the question with a small smile of satisfaction. It seemed that he was anxious to conduct a defence case by getting a quick confession of guilt.

'Is it so terrible? I don't find girls who might wish

to make love to me in the usual course of my every-day life. That's why I ring the telephone numbers. Not too often, though. It comes expensive.'

While Ballard was digesting this reply, I asked the question which, in my view, was the reason for our visit. 'Did you kill Ludmilla Ravenskaya?'

'Of course not! I'm sure she was a lovely girl. But when I saw her, she was dead.'

'All right,' I carried on while my learned leader was shuffling his papers. 'So you say the maid, this Miss McKinnan, told you to go into the sitting room and wait for a short while. Then if Ludmilla didn't come out to you, you were to knock on the bedroom door and go in to her.'

'Yes, that's what she said. Well, I waited in the sitting room and read some magazines that she had lying about. Then, after ten minutes, I knocked at the bedroom door. There was no answer, so I pushed the door open. Then I saw her.'

'Alive?'

'No, Mr Rumpole. Dead.'

'Did you know that then?'

'I didn't know. But I saw the marks on her throat. The bed was untidy. There was a table knocked over, as though there'd been some sort of a struggle. So I called for the maid —'

'McKinnan?'

'She accused me straight away. She accused me of killing the girl.'

'And then?'

'She told me to stay there. She went out and locked the sitting-room door. So I was a prisoner. It was then she called the police.'

'That's what she says. How long was it before the police arrived?'

'Quite a while. I suppose an hour, maybe more.'

It was at this point that my not quite so learned leader, who had been looking increasingly depressed and disapproving as I asked a few penetrating questions, came in with, 'Mr Rumpole has gone into the details, Wetherby, but I have to look at the big picture. The point remains that the woman Ravenskaya was seen alive before your visit and during your visit she was found dead. You were the only person with her at this time. You must realize that we can hold out very little hope in your case.'

I thought it was far too early to reach such a verdict, so I said, 'Until I've cross-examined the prosecution witnesses, including the forensic expert, we can't say that there is *no* hope.'

'You seem to have forgotten, Rumpole,' Soapy

Sam reminded the meeting, 'that the duty of cross-examining the prosecution witnesses will fall on me.'

'Then perhaps there *is* no hope after all,' I thought, but I restrained myself from saying it.

'I'm seriously worried about Wetherby,' Sam Ballard told me as we walked out of the prison gate.

'Don't give up all hope,' I said, and advised him to have a careful look at the post-mortem photographs.

'It's not that, Rumpole. But should a silk in my position at the Bar, with my reputation for complete moral probity, be concerned in this extremely squalid murder? Added to that, as Chair-elect of the Lawyers as Christians Society, should I be defending a client who has lost all sense of decency and become a frequenter of brothels?'

I would like to have said, 'That's exactly why he needs defending', but I didn't. I remained silent, and I now saw some blessed hope arising from Sam Ballard's strong sense of moral repugnance.

7

Rumpole, QC. As I say, Queer Customers is what I always call them, and no doubt they'd be calling me that; but there are so many queer customers who have attained the rewards of senior barristers, a silk gown and a seat in the front row, that one more shouldn't make much difference. I remembered what Bonny Bernard had said about this most unassuming of men accused of manual strangulation: he wanted a QC to defend him. Even Hilda had wondered why, after so many years at the Bar, I had not reached the front row. I tried saying 'Rumpole, QC' again and found that it had rather a distinguished ring to it.

In the good old days – well, there were *some* good things about them – a barrister with a longing for a silk gown had only to get a couple of judges to write up to the Lord Chancellor, who as head judge easily found out who got drunk in court, or ate peas with his knife, or would date a woman on the jury, and indeed anything else likely to let down the high standards of the front bench.

Times, of course, have changed and nowadays it seems there must be a committee for everything, including sorting out the list of applicants for the silk gown. There are still written reports to the Lord Chancellor, who has incidentally been re-moved from his time-honoured task of supervising the debates in the House of Lords from the Wool-sack, appropriately dressed in a wig, knee breeches, a gown and silk stockings. Now the poor chap has been siphoned off to something called the Ministry of the Constitution or some such title, where, for all I know, he shows up in jeans, a T-shirt and an elderly anorak. He has, I suppose, to follow the whims of the committee in the choice of who to dress in silk.

Meanwhile, I had to call on a platoon of judges,

clients and solicitors to back the Rumpole application. I had no illusions about the difficulty of this task. So far as many people in the top echelon of the legal profession were concerned, my face still didn't fit, and even though I could think of many less fit faces peering out above silk gowns, this was, as I had to explain to Hilda, owing to my determination to get my clients a fair run.

It was a tricky situation, but God, or whatever means the good, came to my assistance. My run of luck started with an unpromising case of dangerous driving in Potters Bar. There was the usual argument about the accuracy of speed cameras and the inaccuracy of police evidence, but the important thing was the prosecutor, a certain Matthew Wickstead, a tall, forbidding bird with a pronounced Adam's apple, a thin beak of a nose and the sort of voice better suited to a church service than the Potters Bar Magistrates' Court.

After my client had been convicted, this Wickstead approached me in a friendly fashion and said, 'You're in Samuel Ballard, QC's chambers, aren't you?'

'Yes.' I had to admit it.

'He's possibly the next Chairman of the Lawyers

as Christians Society. He's on the committee of course. He gives of his time so generously. I shall certainly vote for him as Chair. Do you see much of him?'

'Quite a lot. He's leading me in a case of murder at the moment.'

'A worthy cause? Samuel Ballard's always fighting for worthy causes.'

'Not all that worthy, I'm afraid.' I tried to sound disapproving. 'He's defending a client who went to a brothel. He's alleged to have killed a prostitute. Manual strangulation.'

'Oh dear!' This appeared to be Matthew Wickstead's equivalent of 'What the hell!' 'Samuel Ballard, QC's defending a man who resorts to fallen women?'

'I'm afraid so.'

'And a man who, far from trying to restart and reform, killed one of them?'

'That's what's alleged.'

'Oh, dear me!' Wickstead continued to lament. 'I left the Church and came to the Bar to support worthy causes.'

Was prosecuting a fast driver on the M25 a worthy cause? I supposed so and didn't argue the point, because of what he next said. 'I can scarcely believe that Samuel Ballard, QC, would defend a man who resorts to fallen women.'

'You mean,' I said, determined to clarify the situation, 'the Lawyers as Christians would disapprove of anyone undertaking Graham Wetherby's case?'

'I'm afraid,' Wickstead told me, 'we at LAC would be deeply disappointed.'

'Thank you,' I said. 'That's all I wanted to know.' And so I left him.

It was a sharp, spring morning some weeks later, with a wind that sent our trouser legs flapping and into which we leaned forward like skaters, when Soapy Sam Ballard and I were on our way back from the Old Bailey, where a judge had fixed a date for Graham Wetherby's trial and we had agreed rather more of the facts than I should have liked with the prosecution.

As we walked, I chucked a few well-chosen words into the wind. 'I was against a friend of yours a while back. Matthew Wickstead.'

'Splendid fellow! We serve together on the board of LAC.'

'He mentioned that. He has great respect for you. In fact, he said he'd vote for you as Chair.'

'How was he? Keeping well?'

'He seemed perfectly healthy. Only, I'm afraid, a little sad, a trifle distressed.'

'Not ill, I hope.'

'Not ill, but worried. Not to put too fine a point on it, he was worried about you, Ballard.'

'About me? I hope you reassured him. I'm perfectly well.'

'Oh, it wasn't your health, Ballard. Quite frankly, he was distressed to hear what you're doing.'

'Doing our work?'

'Yes, but what *sort* of work?'

'Leading you in a murder case.'

'That's true.' I had to admit it reluctantly. 'But what *sort* of a case? Defending a man who frequents prostitutes and is supposed to have strangled one of them. *Not* the sort of work for a potential Chair of LAC.'

'Is that what he said?' Ballard stood still now, troubled in the wind.

'Words to that effect.'

Ballard thought for a while and then struck a note of resignation.

'I can't get out of it now.'

'I don't see why not.'

'I can't tell the client it's not the sort of case I should be concerned with.'

'You'll have to say you're engaged elsewhere – you'll have to be sure that there is someone else thoroughly capable of taking it on.'

'Whom might I suggest?'

'Me, of course.' Perhaps it was the wind, but my unlearned leader seemed more than unusually slow on the uptake.

'You feel you could do it?'

'Hopeless cases are my speciality.'

'Perhaps that's what should be done.' Ballard seemed to make up his mind and stepped purposefully forward into the wind. 'Thank you, Rumpole.'

'Oh, don't thank me. Always willing to help. But if you're really grateful, there's a little thing you could do for me.'

'All right. What is it?'

'I'm thinking of applying for a silk gown and a seat in the front row. Would you support my application?'

'You a QC, Rumpole?' He was grinning broadly. 'What a novel suggestion! Well! We'll have to see about that, won't we?'

He seemed to be laughing as he strode on. I let him go. I had *R.* v. *Wetherby* under my belt and I mustn't be greedy.

8

'So has Mr Ballard found a chap in deeper trouble than me?'

'It's not that, Mr Wetherby.' Bonny Bernard spoke with the tone of someone giving an official explanation which he didn't entirely believe to be true. 'Mr Ballard has another commitment which he couldn't get out of.'

'So that means I'm not going to have a QC defend me?'

'You may well have. Mr Rumpole here has applied for a silk gown. I hope that I may be able to mark the brief for Horace Rumpole, QC.' Again I was disturbed by a lack of conviction in Bonny Bernard's tone of voice.

'I have no doubt that I shall be in the front bench when your trial comes on.' I adopted a positive tone to reassure the client. 'I don't see how they can possibly refuse me. My career, ever since the Penge Bungalow Murders, has made me a legend in the Courts of Law.'

'You're sure they'll make you a QC?' The client still didn't sound entirely convinced.

'Just as sure as I am that you're coming on for trial at the Old Bailey. Speaking of which, perhaps you can help me by answering some simple questions.'

We were back again in the interview room in Brixton Prison, with its bare table, its cactus wilting on the window sill and its officer posted on the other side of the door to make sure that there was no sort of dash for freedom. The meeting had begun by our client refusing Bernard's offer of a cigarette, a normal way of putting prisoners at ease, with a long lecture on the dangers of smoking. An odd sort of attitude, I thought, from a man accused of inflicting the far greater danger of manual strangulation.

'You're sure you're going to get the QC?'

'As I say, I don't see how they can refuse me.'

There was a silence, during which Graham Wetherby was no doubt considering whether he could share this optimistic view of Rumpole's future. At last he said, 'All right then. What do you want to know?'

'That mark on your face. Have you had it since you were a child?'

He was sitting by the window, so the swollen red stain was clearly visible. Now he put up a hand to cover it.

'Since I was born, yes.' He explained carefully as though to an imbecile. 'That's why it's called a birthmark.'

'You think that's why girls don't like you?'

'What do you mean, they don't like me?'

'Why they don't want to go to bed with you.'

'I never ask them.'

'Why not?'

'Because I know what they'd say.'

'So it's because of the mark on your face that all your experience of sex has been with prostitutes.'

'They don't mind about it. Not if you can pay them enough.'

'So let's say you'd had a number of girls who were

on the game for, let's say, at least the last ten years?'

'For as long as I could afford it.'

'Then let's say for about the last five years?'

'About that – yes.'

'And did anything like this ever happen before?'

'That I killed any of them? No. Of course it didn't happen. I keep telling you. What've I got?' Graham Wetherby turned angrily to Bonny Bernard. 'What've you got for me? A brief, not even a QC, who thinks I'm guilty. I always strangle them, is that what he thinks?'

'I think nothing of the sort.' I did my best to quieten the client. 'To me you're innocent until the jury comes back and tells me otherwise. What I really want to know is, had you ever been locked in a sitting room before, on your previous visits to them?'

'Never. No, that never happened. Not that I can recall.'

I made a note on my brief and then asked the final question.

'And just tell me. How close did you get to her? When you discovered she was dead?'

There was a silence in the small, closely guarded room before he answered. 'I kissed her.' And then, while his legal advisers remained silent, he said,

John Mortimer

'They don't do kissing. Those types of girls. Not when they're alive.'

The familiar interview room seemed cold and I felt an unusual sadness in the presence of the pale young man with the funny cheek who only received a kiss from the dead. Then I pulled myself together and gave some instructions to my solicitor.

'Get on to Professor Andrew Ackerman,' I told Bonny Bernard. 'Get him to hurry up and give us a report on the post-mortem findings and photographs. Oh, and I suppose we might get some sort of a character reference.' I turned to the client. 'I understand you work at the Home Office. In which department?'

'I used to be in youth crimes – juvenile delinquency.'

I thought of the youth crime I was dealing with, the little matter of a thoughtlessly kicked football, a million miles away from the adult offence which had brought me to Brixton.

'But I was moved last year. A new post – seconded to a new department.'

'Your boss there,' I asked him, 'would he speak up for you?'

'There are so many of us there. I don't really know my boss.'

53

'Well, Mr Bernard will see what he can do. I think that's all for the moment.'

'Just one thing, Mr Rumpole. You say you're getting a QCship?'

'It's in the pipeline.' I did my best to reassure him.

'You think it'll come through in time for my trial?'

'Let's hope so. But even if it doesn't you'll have the best service available at the Old Bailey.'

'From you, Mr Rumpole?'

'And from no one else.'

'I'd just feel satisfied in my mind if I could have a QC there for this occasion.'

He had kissed a dead girl, he was up on a charge of murder with a defence which was not yet entirely clear, and his only worry seemed to be the quality of my gown and whether or not I might be seated in the front or second row.

As we parted he brought the matter up again. 'Please, Mr Rumpole,' he said. 'Couldn't you manage to speed it up?'

'You mean the trial?'

'No, sir. I mean your QC.'

My wife, Hilda, was back from the bridge club early that afternoon and, instead of her usual reliving of some of the more dramatic hands and sad tales of how she had just missed three No Trumps because of her partner's ineptitude, that evening she seemed to be taking an unusual interest in the law.

'Of course provocation would reduce the crime of murder to manslaughter,' She Who Must stated. 'Was there no provocation in the Wetherby case?'

'Not really. He says the girl was dead.'

'Of course he would say that, wouldn't he? They all do.'

'Who are "they all"?'

'Everyone in that type of situation.' Hilda seemed to be speaking of her vast experience. 'How's his mentality?'

'Pretty worried at the moment, I should say.'

'You know what I mean, Rumpole.' Hilda was getting impatient 'Has he a classified mental disease? Is he unhinged? Mentally deficient?'.

'I suppose so, seeing as he works for the Home Office.'

'Oh, do be serious, Rumpole! What I mean is, as I'm sure you realize, could he go for diminished responsibility?'

'I hardly think so. He seemed to be perfectly bright, for a civil servant.'

'It's saying things like that, Rumpole,' Hilda's

tone was serious, 'that so irritates judges. You want to avoid those little jokes you're so full of. They don't do you any good at all. No provocation. No diminished responsibility. I'll have to give *R.* v. *Wetherby* some more serious thought.'

'That's very kind of you, Hilda,' I felt I had to say.

'Not at all. Of course I'm anxious to prevent your practice going totally to pieces. You can tell Wetherby that I'm giving his case some serious thought.'

'That's very big of you.'

'It's good to have a practical case to work on.'

'I'm sure. But there's only one thing my client is really worried about.'

'What's that?'

'He wants me to become a QC. He really wants to be defended by a silk.'

'Really? And have you agreed to that, Rumpole?'

'The thought had crossed my mind.'

'If you got it you'll be put at the level of Daddy.'

'That would be an honour.' My fingers were crossed. My late father-in-law's performances in court didn't improve when he became a QC.

'Let me put my mind to it,' Hilda said again as she was serving out the lamb chops, frozen peas and boiled potatoes. 'We'll see what we shall see.'

Though I asked her for further particulars of her last remark she clammed up, and we had no more discussion about the law for the rest of the evening.

9

Extract from the Memoirs of Hilda Rumpole

Rumpole, who in my opinion has been mouldering for far too long as about the oldest junior at the Criminal Bar, seems to have come to his senses at last and decided to pull himself up by his own bootstraps. He has at last decided to apply for silk. Of course Rumpole will never be as distinguished a QC as Daddy – to whom Rumpole's murder cases seemed very downmarket when compared with his speciality in property rights, contracts and bills of exchange. At least no one had to die to provide my father with work. I think, however, Daddy would have been pleased that I at least had a husband who was entitled to put the letters QC after his name.

I first knew of Rumpole's decision when Leonard Bullingham, after we had bid and won a satisfying four Hearts, pulled a crumpled letter from out of his pocket. 'A letter from your old man,' Leonard told me. 'Hardly the most tactful way of asking for a favour, is it?'

He gave me the letter in question for inclusion in these very memoirs, so I am able to quote it in its entirety. It began, as I thought, in a way that hovered between the overly familiar and the downright rude.

My dear Old Bull

My wife may have told you, during the course of one of those tedious card games you both appear to enjoy, that I'm thinking of putting on a silk gown and joining those QCs (Queer Customers is what I call them) who loll around the front row in various courtrooms relying on their underpaid 'juniors' to do all the hard work. In support of my application I need to call a client and a judge who can speak well of me.

As a client I can call any member of the Timson family whom I may have rescued, by my skill as an advocate, from the shades of the prison house. Finding a decent criminal is easy. It's harder to find a judge who would be equally helpful. Looking back on the cases I did before you at the Old Bailey, I feel sure that you would be pleased to admit that my arguments were, on the whole, arguments based on the interests of justice, so I feel sure I can rely on your support for my present application.

Your old sparring partner,

Horace Rumpole

PS I'm sure my wife would welcome your support for the Rumpole case. She has wondered why my undoubted talent as an advocate has not yet elevated me to the same rank as her late father. It's for her sake that I have had to plead this most difficult of all cases – my own.

'What are you going to do about Rumpole's letter?' I asked Leonard after I had read it.

'Put it in the bin for recycling. It might emerge as a decent bit of toilet paper.' Rumpole's letter seemed to have brought out the cruder side of Leonard.

'He does say you had legal arguments . . .'

'Nonsense. They weren't legal arguments. They were . . . ploys drummed up by your husband with the purpose of getting the jury to dislike me.'

Leonard looked pained as he said this, so I felt I had to cheer him up. I said, 'I'm sure he never succeeded in doing that.'

'Sometimes he did. I think sometimes he made the jury think I was a direct descendant of Judge Jeffreys, dead set on a conviction.' I was quite touched by Leonard when he said that. He was looking at me in the way of a small boy left out of the football team, pleading for reassurance.

'No jury would ever think that when they got to know you, Leonard.'

'Dear Hilda.' Here he put his hand on mine across the bridge table, where we sat alone for a while after Mash and her partner had gone off to see about the tea. 'You are such a wonderful consolation to a man.'

'I try to be,' I said.

'I can't ask a whole jury to meet me for tea and bridge. So Rumpole's perverse view of my character is never challenged.'

'It does seem terribly unfair.'

'But I have one great consolation.'

'What's that?'

'I can tell you about my troubles.'

'Any time.' His hand seemed particularly weighty at that moment, so I took mine away. 'You told me that when you become a QC you rule yourself out from all the smaller, less important cases.'

'Let's say you're no longer offered the bread and butter. You're kept for the caviar and roast goose.'

'So Rumpole wouldn't be able to deal with all the petty crimes the Timson family get up to?'

'Certainly not. Such minor offences by the south London riff-raff wouldn't be considered worth the expensive employment of a leading QC.'

It was when he said this that I became thoughtful. 'But people like the Timsons and so on – they will still need defending?'

'Of course. They'd be on the lookout for another junior.'

'It might be someone who'd only recently been called to the Bar?'

It was then that Leonard looked at me in some surprise. 'Hilda,' he said, 'can I guess what you are thinking?'

'I'm thinking,' I told him, 'that you should do all you can to help Rumpole to become a QC.'

10

'A woman came to see me about young Peter.'
Bertie Timson spoke with some amazement.

We had met in Pommeroy's, my favourite wine
bar. I had organized a meeting there with Dennis,
at that time the head and undisputed leader of the
Timson clan and with whom, after an unhappy
difference of opinion when I was defending Dr
Khan on a charge of terrorism, I was back again on
friendly terms. He had turned up in the company
of Bertie, who delayed the matter of business by

describing the joys of parenthood during the dying years of the now deeply caring government. I passed a glass of Château Thames Embankment to silence him but he had a strange story which clearly had to be told.

'She said she was a "state nanny" and she had been selected to advise me on parenting, seeing that young Peter had an ASBO.'

'I'm sorry about that. It hurts me to remember our unsuccessful defence.'

'No. Peter's very grateful for what you've done for him, Mr Rumpole. He really is. He's ever so proud of the ASBO.'

'He's got to be careful now,' I warned his father. 'The present government's dead keen on putting children behind bars.'

'Perhaps that's why she wanted me to do "parenting".'

'Did you get to understand what she was talking about?' Dennis seemed mystified.

'Well, she asked if I read to him in bed. And I told her I didn't. So she left me a book. Something about a bear that kept taking honey. Not very exciting reading, I didn't think. But she said if I read to Peter in bed regular, it'd keep him from going into the nick.'

'Did you try it?' Dennis seemed unable to get enough of this story.

'When he was in bed. Yes. I sat down and started to read out about this bear liking honey. Oh, and there was a boy in it with a picture of him wearing shorts.'

'How did your Peter take it?'

'He said, "Shut up, Dad. I'm listening to my iPod." It was the iPod you gave him at Christmas time.'

'That's all we find in houses nowadays. IPods and sound systems. No one keeps money any more.' Dennis was nostalgic for the good old days. 'What else did she tell you to do?'

'She asked if I had ever sung to him. She never said what sort of songs. Ones we sung down the pub – I didn't think she'd like them. So I said no, I didn't go in for singing.'

'Bertie sang down the pub,' Dennis confided in me. 'It was horrible.'

'She asked about "Ring a ring o' roses" ... that sort of thing. I did try that after tea once. My Leonie said she'd leave me if ever I did that again. So the state nanny wasn't all that help as it turned out. You were the only one that tried to help, Mr Rumpole. For which we are very grateful.'

'Any time!' I had lit a small cigar and now waved it casually in the air. 'Call on me at any time. I'm always as ready to help young Peter as I am to help any member of the Timson family.'

After I had refilled their glasses Dennis said, 'I thought we'd come here so the Timson family could help you?'

'Well, that's right,' I had to admit. 'You see, I decided that it was high time I put on a silk gown and got promoted to the front row in court.'

'You mean you want Queen's Counsel?' A long life in and out of the Old Bailey had given Dennis Timson a sound working knowledge of the law.

'You're right,' I told him. 'And I need a judge and a satisfied client to speak up for me.'

Dennis thought this over for a moment, gave himself another swig and came up with, 'You'll be hard put to find a judge, won't you, Mr Rumpole? They're not too keen on the way you keep winning cases.'

'Surprisingly enough,' I told him, 'Mr Justice Leonard Bullingham has offered his services.'

'Him you used to call the Mad Bull?'

'Exactly. He seems to have come to his senses. So could I rely on you to say . . . well, that I've always done my best for my clients? I suppose that's what they want to hear.'

'QC.' Dennis repeated the magical letters thoughtfully. 'We don't get a QC doing most of our family's cases.'

'Petty thefts, minor break-ins, selling stolen fish and all that sort of thing. You're quite right,' I admitted to Dennis. 'I shouldn't be able to do them. But I'm sure you'll find a satisfactory junior. And when it comes to the bigger stuff . . .'

'What bigger stuff is that, Mr Rumpole?'

'Bank robberies. Serious frauds. Or let's say "a murder". Not that I'm encouraging you to commit any such crimes, of course.'

'No, of course not, Mr Rumpole. That is clearly understood.' There was something entirely judicial about the silence that followed. Dennis was clearly having some trouble making up his mind. At last he came out with, 'All right, Mr Rumpole. Taking all that into consideration, I am prepared to speak up for you.'

'Thank you, Dennis.' I was genuinely grateful. 'It's very good of you and exactly what I would expect from a senior member of the Timson family. All you need to tell them is that I always did my best for you – even in difficult cases.'

'Rely on me, Mr Rumpole. And I'll keep quiet about the cases when your best wasn't quite good enough.'

'You mean the cases when the prosecution had you bang to rights? Well, I suppose that's fair enough. Now, I think the tide's gone down in our glasses.'

When I had arranged matters with Jack Pommeroy and added the cost of another round to my hope for the arrival of another legal aid cheque, I noticed Bertie Timson smiling, apparently at the memory of some private joke.

'What's so funny about Mr Rumpole going after a QC?' Dennis asked him.

'It's not that. But when you said "cases", it reminded me about the trouble old Scottie Thompson got into. Only it's crates with him, not cases. I reckon Scottie'll be coming to you for advice, Mr Rumpole.'

'Then I'll do my best for him. What's his trouble exactly?'

'Illegal immigration. Scottie's got his own long-distance lorry. Runs it as a freelancer. He got a call from this firm that was apparently in trouble with its transport and had some crates needed picking up in some crazy place. Eastern Europe, I think that's where it was.'

'So what was the trouble?' I was curious to know.

'Well, you won't believe this. He picked up the crates, three big ones like new. He got as far as Dover with them, when there was some sort of inspection of the cargo. It seems there was a noise from one of the crates.'

'What sort of noise?'

'I don't know. Perhaps a girl crying, because what happened when they opened the crates up – he'd brought girls hid in crates, Scottie said. Course, he told them he knew nothing about it, but would they believe him? Course not! You'll have a job getting him off, I reckon.'

'If your friend Scottie asks for me, tell him I'll do my best.'

Dennis was laughing at Bertie's story but I couldn't see the joke. All I could think of was a journey across Europe, nailed up in a packing case. Human beings exported like so many jars of mango chutney.

I I

Briefs are, I have always thought, very like the number 11 bus. You wait an age to get one and then a whole platoon of them turn up at the same time. Not too long ago I had been facing unemployment, enforced retirement and the prospect of long days without wig or gown in the sole company of She Who Must Be Obeyed in Froxbury Mansions. Now I had not only young Peter's ASBO and Graham Wetherby's murder but also, thanks again to the industrious Bonny Bernard,

Scottie Thompson's importation of illegal female immigrants by way of the port of Dover.

I was brooding over the defence in the last-named case when there was a sharp rap on the door and there entered Claude Erskine-Brown. I heard the voice but didn't turn my head to it.

'I've come to serve you, Rumpole,' was what he said.

'That's extremely kind of you, Erskine-Brown. I'd like a large cup of black coffee, no milk or sugar, and a couple of Chambers shortbread biscuits.'

'I don't mean I've come to serve you, Rumpole. Rather I'm here to serve *on* you.'

'Please, Erskine-Brown. I'm sure there was a laugh in there somewhere, but as you can see I'm extremely busy. An important immigration case has come my way. It will probably hit the headlines. So if you can give me the coffee without delay . . .'

'I am not serving you coffee, Rumpole. And I understand shortbread biscuits are no longer available. I am serving *this* on you now, and I'd like you to sign on the form that you've received it.'

For the first time I turned to look at the chap. He was holding out a piece of paper which seemed to quiver in his shaking hand. Erskine-Brown was, I thought, in a state of high excitement. I took the paper from him and spread it out on my desk. 'What's this, Claude?' I tried to be civil. 'Another slice of criminal law the government's produced which no one can understand?'

'Read it, Rumpole. I think you'll find it perfectly understandable.'

I glanced at the document. It seemed to bear my name and I read a heading: 'Application for an Anti-social Behaviour Order'. I thought it must have something to do with the case of young Peter Timson until I read the particulars of the conduct complained of. They came in a column headed 'Behaviour of Horace Rumpole', which I will quote in full for accuracy.

1. Bringing various articles of food into Chambers such as portions of cold steak and kidney pie, various cheeses, cooked sausages and chipped potatoes. On several occasions a shepherd's pie would be imported from a public house and gradually consumed over a period of days. On several occasions uneaten portions of this pie were discovered left in a filing cabinet in the said Rumpole's room expressly provided for the storage of legal documents.

2. Bringing intoxicating drinks into the said Chambers such as bottles of wine and consuming them on the premises.

3. On several occasions singing in his room in the said Chambers, thereby causing embarrassment to the members and the clerical staff.

4. Smoking small cigars causing a health hazard in Chambers and further polluting the atmosphere and thereby increasing the risk of global warming.

'Who thought up this ridiculous document?' I asked Claude after I had read it through.

'We have formed a sub-committee to deal with your behaviour, Rumpole.'

'Oh, have you indeed? And is Soapy Sam in any way connected with this rubbish?'

'Samuel Ballard, QC, has given us his blessing.'

'Oh, has he indeed? What ingratitude!'

'It's not just our leader, Rumpole. The staff of the chambers have told us that firm steps must be taken to see that you become more environmentally friendly. Now, if you'll consent to sign along the dotted lines . . .'

'Consent? I'm not consenting to anything. I may eat steak and kidney pie, I may seek comfort in Pommeroy's Very Ordinary, I may need a small cigar. *You* may feed on nut cutlets and drink carrot juice enlivened with a few bubbles. But I know which of us a client would rather have on his side when the dark shadows of the law begin to close in against him. So that's what I think of your ridiculous bit of paper.' At this I tore the so-called legal document Claude had attempted to serve on me into small fragments, which I tipped into my wastepaper basket.

'That was very foolish of you, Rumpole.' Claude spoke more in sorrow than in anger. 'I can prove service of the notice and the law will have to take its course.'

Claude withdrew and I sat back in my chair. I thought I could understand how young Peter Timson felt when he was hauled up in court for kicking a football down a street. He must have experienced a strong desire to go on kicking it. I went over to the cabinet to unearth the bottle of Château Thames Embankment I kept filed under the XYZs for emergencies. I drew the cork and, having filled a glass, drank a silent toast to anti-social behaviour. Then I came to my senses. I had something far more serious to concentrate on. A new brief had arrived in the case I had learned of in Pommeroy's a few weeks before from my client, the ASBO boy's father. It was the affair of Scottie Thompson and his unintentional importation of Russian beauties.

I 2

So many cases have started in the interview room in Brixton Prison that the place has become a sort of home from home. It was there that I met Scottie Thompson. He was a short, high-shouldered, perpetually smiling man who seemed very anxious to please. When I asked him where he came from north of the border, it turned out that he was not really a Scot, but had so much enjoyed a holiday tour of the Highlands, and had talked about it so much, that his friends had named him Scottie. He had set up a business named, of course, Highlands Transport.

Scottie had known Fred Atkins since they were at school together. He knew that Fred drove a lot over in Europe for what he said was an 'import and export company'. Fred had a pick-up job in Europe on the day of his daughter's wedding, and Scottie was not particularly surprised when his friend asked him to do it for him.

'He gave me the paperwork and all that. I couldn't see no problem and it was good pay. Fred gave me the lot.'

I asked him where he picked up the crates.

'Romanian border. I had a meet there. The man said he'd brought the load over from Russia. Said he couldn't drive the load to Dover "because they knew him too well". I didn't quite know what he meant by that.'

'Did you know then where you were supposed to be taking them?'

'Fred had told me to deliver at a warehouse in the Canary Wharf area. I was to ring him when I'd got through Customs.'

'And did you ring him?'

'Yes. I could hear the sounds of the wedding party. I was talking to him when Customs were opening the crates. I told him what was happening and he slammed the phone down on me. Never heard a word from him since. It was then that I saw what I'd brought over. Girls, good-lookers too. They must have had a terrible journey. I wanted to find out more, but I got arrested.'

'And Fred?'

'He's done a runner.'

'We've given all this information to the police,' Bonny Bernard told me. 'There's a search on for Fred. All the ports and airports.'

'So the opening of the crates came as a complete surprise to you?'

'I'd never have done it if I knew, Mr Rumpole. That's no way to make a woman travel, no way at all.'

I looked at Scottie. He seemed puzzled, bewildered. But then his smile was almost proud.

'They got me for the mastermind, have they, Mr Rumpole?'

'We'll try to prove that you weren't, that you were an entirely innocent cog in a complicated piece of machinery.'

'Oh, is that all I was?' Scottie looked almost disappointed.

Did I believe him? I told myself firmly that it

didn't matter what I believed, a jury would have to decide.

So we left Brixton Prison and a client who seemed to regret he would never make a serious criminal. He was just someone who, like the girls in the crates, had been taken for a ride.

13

A week or two later I was contemplating with some satisfaction the current state of the Rumpole career: an important murder in Court Number One at the Old Bailey, from which I had managed to remove the unwelcome assistance of my not so learned leader, and the curious case of the crated women. I treated myself to a couple of ham sandwiches and had just opened my private bottle of Pommeroy's Very Ordinary when, like a dark cloud flitting across a sunlit sky, my ex-leader appeared in the doorway.

'Rumpole!' Sam Ballard's greeting was not altogether friendly. 'You're doing it *again*.'

'Oh yes. I manage to keep going somehow. A number of important cases in the pipeline. There's a satisfactory number of persons who still need Rumpole. And I'm perfectly willing to oblige.'

'I'm not talking about your criminal practice, Rumpole. I speak of your repeated anti-social behaviour. You've brought food in here again, Rumpole, you're bringing alcoholic drink into Chambers, and when you finish your picnic I've no doubt that you'll be tempted to smoke one of those unhealthy little cigars you still carry about with you.'

'I have every intention,' I told him, 'of yielding to that temptation.'

'Not for much longer! The government will soon see to that.'

Ballard sighed heavily, looked at me in a despairing sort of way and plonked himself down in my client's chair.

'I'm here to help you, Rumpole, to help and advise you. Now, wasn't it very foolish of you to avoid service of the ASBO?'

'I couldn't take it seriously.'

'You'll have to take it seriously.'

'The serious thing about ASBOs is that they're an outrage to our great legal system. A boy kicking a football can be sent to prison for conduct which is not a crime after not having had a fair trial with the presumption of innocence. The boy either wears his ASBO like a badge of honour or goes to prison, where he can learn to be a serious crook.'

'Rumpole, you must move with the times.'

'If I don't like the way the times are moving I shall refuse to accompany them.'

'Very well then.' Ballard slapped his knees and hinged himself out of my chair. 'You can expect service of another document.'

'And what about your behaviour?'

'What do you mean?'

'Telling my solicitor Bonny Bernard that you couldn't do the murder case because of a previous engagement when in truth you'd taken a hearty dislike to young Wetherby and all his doings.'

Ballard stood silent for a moment then said, 'The solicitors don't know that, do they?'

'Not yet. But they may do if we hear any more about this ASBO business.'

There was a long pause. Ballard heaved a sigh and made his way to the door. 'I'll have to consult all our members. Some of them were very keen on the idea.'

So he left me. I have to admit that I felt a pang of guilt. Had the criminal instincts of my clients rubbed off on me and was I guilty of blackmail? I dismissed the thought on the grounds that all is fair in love and ASBOs, then I finished my glass of Pommeroy's Very Ordinary.

14

'Listen! you hear the grating roar
Of pebbles which the waves draw back, and fling,
At their return, up the high strand . . .'

'What's that all about?' Bonny Bernard looked puzzled.

'A poem by Matthew Arnold. Son of a boring headmaster who invented the public-school system. Dover beach meant almost as much to him as it does to us.'

I had persuaded my instructing solicitor to drive

me to the coast on a Saturday morning to do some essential research on the Wetherby case. We were at the harbour, looking down at the sea.

'We've got to discover more about Ludmilla. People usually have some reason for getting themselves murdered.'

'She died because Wetherby found strangling another way of having sex.' Bonny Bernard always took a pessimistic view of his clients.

'Do you believe that? Graham Wetherby had been visiting prostitutes for years, him and his birthmark, without resorting to violence.'

'That may be true. But what do you want to know about the girl?'

'Ludmilla? She came from Russia. Scottie Thompson told us about a delivery of girls from Russia in crates.'

'You're suggesting that Scottie had Ludmilla in the back of his lorry?'

'Probably not. That would be too much of a coincidence. But she may have used the same method of transport. Do you know how Matthew Arnold finished his poem?'

'Not yet, Mr Rumpole, but I'm sure you're going to tell me.'

'And we are here as on a darkling plain
Swept with confused alarms of struggle and flight,
Where ignorant armies clash by night.'

'I don't know what that's got to do with it.'
'That's what's happening today, isn't it? Ignorant armies clashing everywhere. And lost people running away in search of new homes, safety and regular money. Look! This is where they are unloading the lorries. I wonder how many uninvited guests they've brought in today.'
'Where are we going now?'
'In search of beer and a sandwich.'
'No more poetry?'
'No more, I promise.'
We went to a harbour bar, a place full of pale, anxious families about to go on holiday, and suntanned happier travellers arriving home.
'We're going to the Removal Centre next.' I was enjoying a pint of Guinness and a double-decker sandwich.
'What on earth is the Removal Centre?'
'Where they either decide to keep you here or, far more frequently, force you to go back to where you came from. It'd be interesting to see how Ludmilla slipped through their fingers.'

'It won't take too long?'

'Of course not.'

'I told my wife that I was just taking you out for a short spin in the country.'

'As the barrister of your choice, Bonny Bernard,' I told him, 'I am responsible for many things, but not for what you tell your wife. Drink up now and we can get going.'

The Removal Centre was a large, not particularly friendly looking building near to the harbour. It was clearly full to overflowing, with the sounds of children crying, women protesting and men arguing in various languages.

We were shown into an office stuffed with computers, presided over by an unsmiling woman who looked as though she wanted us to be removed without any further delay. I told her that we were lawyers engaged on an important case 'funded by the government'. I asked her if she could discover whether someone called Ludmilla Ravenskaya entered the country on the date when Scottie's crates were opened, and she was delighted to tell me that there was no record of her having done so. We were about to be dismissed when God, having nothing better to do, came to the aid of a struggling defence barrister. I heard the cry of 'Mr Rumpole' and turned to see a face I vaguely recognized, pink-cheeked and decorated with a small moustache.

'Don't you remember? I'm Des Pershore of the M2. They wanted to do me for dangerous driving a couple of years ago.'

Fragments of memory returned, another argument about the reliability of speed cameras and some contradictory police evidence.

'Didn't I get you off?'

'Indeed you did, Mr Rumpole! If I'd got a conviction my life wouldn't have been worth living. I work here now. So, what can I do for you?'

'They say they are on a case funded by the government.' The woman sounded as though she didn't believe a word of it.

'I'm sure they are. Mr Rumpole is a very important barrister,' Pershore was happy to correct her. 'Now, how can I help you, Mr Rumpole? It would be a small return for all you did for me.'

I told him that I wanted to know if a Russian woman named Ludmilla Ravenskaya had entered the country via Dover.

This led to prolonged clicking research on various computers, which ended in a cry of triumph from Pershore.

'I've got it for you, Mr Rumpole. It was 12 September last year. Illegal entry into Dover harbour.'

'And what happened? Was she sent back to where she came from?'

Pershore was frowning in a puzzled sort of way at one of his machines. 'It seems not. She was allowed to apply for asylum.'

'What does that mean exactly?'

'We let her go free on the condition that she reported regularly to a police station in the Paddington area.'

'Had anyone suggested that she might be a candidate for asylum?'

'I'm afraid the computer doesn't tell you that sort of thing. It seems she was just one of the lucky ones.'

'Not all that lucky.'

'Why?'

'She got herself murdered.'

In the car on the way back Bonny Bernard accused me of deceit. 'You said you were doing a case that the government is paying for.'

'So it is.'

'What do you mean?'

'We're defending Wetherby on legal aid. That's the government's money, isn't it?'

'So you're saying it wasn't a lie?'

'No. Just a slightly misleading statement, but it was for a good cause.'

'What good cause exactly?'

'Finding out who recommended Ludmilla as a candidate for asylum. Who was it who really wanted her here?'

As we pulled up outside Froxbury Mansions some time later, I turned to Bonny Bernard and said, 'Thank you. And thank your good wife for letting us hear the grating roar of pebbles on Dover beach.'

15

'You're to be congratulated,' I told the jury after one of my less interesting engagements, 'on having sat through one of the most boring cases ever heard at the Old Bailey.'

'It may well come as a surprise to you to know,' responded the presiding judge, Sir Leonard Bullingham no less, who couldn't resist putting in his own two pennyworth, 'that it is not the sole purpose of the criminal law of England to entertain Mr Rumpole!'

There were some obedient sniggers from the

jury at this but I thought it was not altogether funny. My life among so many cheerful criminals and vainglorious judges had brought me more pleasure than could ever be experienced by a rock star or record-breaking mountaineer.

At the end of that day in court the usher told me, 'Our judge wants to see you in his room, Mr Rumpole.' So, going behind the scenes, I knocked on His Lordship's door and walked in to find the Mad Bull ducking and diving and throwing punches at the reflection of himself in a mirror fixed to a cupboard door. I watched this, fascinated and in the faint hope that he might land a blow on his own reflection. Then he caught sight of me in the mirror.

'Shadow-boxing, Rumpole. Keep fit, mustn't we? The women expect it of us.'

'Which women exactly?' I was finding it hard to follow His Lordship's drift.

'The lovely Hilda.' I remembered then that the Bull had suggested that She Who Must ought to divorce me and marry him – a suggestion she turned down when he added the condition that they might take dancing lessons together.

'I don't know whether you really understand

this, Rumpole. Your wife has a formidable intellect.'

'Of course I understand. Hilda's no fool.'

'Certainly not! Did you know that girl of yours remembers every card played in a round of bridge? She's got a mind that would get her straight through the Bar exams. No trouble at all.'

'Are you trying to tell me,' I was finding the conversation difficult to grasp, 'that Hilda wants to go to the Bar?'

'Of course.'

'She wants to practise? Where?'

'She would like to practise at the Criminal Bar, Rumpole. Living with you, she knows all about it anyway. Now she's going to be able to put it to good use.'

'What sort of use is that?'

'What's the name of that family you're always representing?'

'The Timsons.'

'The Timsons, yes! With their perpetual troubles – which aren't really serious enough for a silk to be employed. You would be rather relieved if all those cases could be passed on to Hilda. You'll be glad when you've done it.'

'Done what?'

'Taken silk, of course. Hilda will have to go through the Bar exams, but that will be no trouble to a mind like hers!'

'So you received my letter?'

'Rumpole, I have considered your letter long and hard.'

'And are you prepared to recommend me? I need a judge.'

'I know you do – and here I am. I think the name Bullingham will carry a bit of weight with the Department for Constitutional Affairs.'

I want to confess that I was stumped for words. It was as though I had been ready to meet an angry wolfhound, only to discover that my hand was being licked by an almost embarrassingly attentive Pomeranian.

'It's enormously kind of you,' I said.

'Of course it is. Without my name you don't have a cat in hell's chance. The title "High Court Judge" still carries a bit of clout in the corridors of power. And when you've got your silk, Hilda can start firing on all cylinders.'

'Thank you for doing this for me.'

'I'm not doing it for you, Rumpole, I'm doing it for her.'

Going home on the tube from Temple station I

fell into a sleep. In a moment of dreaming, I saw the huge figure of She Who Must Be Obeyed dressed in a wig and gown with her arms full of briefs in cases.

When I got back to Froxbury Mansions, and Hilda was reduced to the normal size, she said, 'Leonard Bullingham tells me he's going to back your claim for silk.'

'He told me that too.'

'I think it's enormously kind of him, considering how rude you've been to him in court.'

'Considering how rude he has been to me in court, it's very good of me to accept his help!'

'Did Leonard tell you I'm thinking of reading for the Bar? He says I have exactly the right talents for it.'

'If that means you can argue the hind legs off a donkey, I have to agree,' was what I didn't say. Hilda had made her decision and I would have to learn to live with it.

A few weeks after the events chronicled above I was seated alone in my favourite corner of Pommeroy's Wine Bar, sharing a bottle of Château Thames Embankment with myself.

At a distant table, presided over by Claude

Erskine-Brown, other members of 4 Equity Court Chambers were gathered. Hoskins, a barrister who had to maintain his many daughters, was there, and my ex-pupil Mizz Liz Probert, and Luci Gribble too, perhaps to look after our image. Even our clerk, Henry, was telling some anecdote, no doubt about Rumpole, which appeared to set the table on a roar. Ever since the attempt to serve an anti-social behaviour order upon me, I had been treated by my fellow members like some ancient and out-dated piece of machinery, a wind-up gramophone perhaps.

Did I, in fact, represent some antique part of Chambers which needed clearing out in the war against global warming?

I was sitting alone with that thought when a sharp voice said, 'Lars Bergman, new crime corre-spondent of the *Daily Fortress*. You're Mr Rumpole, aren't you?'

It was useless to deny it to the youngish man with slicked-down blond hair who immediately sat down at my lonely table uninvited.

'The man at the bar pointed you out. I'm doing a piece on the Wetherby case. Isn't it a funny sort of case for you to be defending?'

'I haven't got many laughs out of it up till now.'

'But it's a hopeless defence, isn't it? I mean, the man is so obviously guilty.'

I refrained from offering Mr Bergman a drink. 'Hopeless cases,' I told him, 'are rather my speciality.'

'That's what my editor objects to.'

'I'm not really doing my work to please your editor.'

'He thinks defending hopeless cases is a shocking waste of public money. This *is* a legal aid case, isn't it?'

'And what does your editor intend to do about it?'

'He thinks a single judge should look at the case, and if there's nothing that amounts to a defence, he could order a short trial.'

'Your editor must be extremely old.'

'A younger man than you are, Mr Rumpole.'

'He's like our present government. All born before 1215, the date of Magna Carta. They haven't yet heard that no one is to be sent to prison without a trial by his equals.'

Bergman looked at me for a moment in a puzzled sort of way, and then he said something which seemed to switch on lights all around him and make him the sole object of interest for me in Pommeroy's Wine Bar.

'I suppose I feel strongly about it,' he said, 'because I met her.'

'You met Ludmilla Ravenskaya?'

'Yes. She told me her name. And it was the same address, off Sussex Gardens.'

'You went there,' here I put it as delicately as I could, 'as a client?'

'Not really. My editor wanted me to write about the organization, whatever it was, which was importing these girls in the backs of lorries.'

'Perhaps I judged your editor too harshly. That's a subject I should love to have investigated.'

'I saw her name up in a telephone box. "Exotic Russian beauty will show you that the Cold War is over". There was a telephone number.'

'So you went to Flyte Street?'

'And met Ludmilla, yes. She thought I'd come for sex, of course, but I told her I'd come for information which would be far better paid.'

'So she told you what exactly?'

'Nothing then. She said she was far too busy with clients, but she told me to call her in a week or two and she'd give me the story. She wanted half the money in advance.'

'Did she get it?'

'No, but I gave her £100 as a retainer. That was

on top of what I had to pay for the sex I didn't have.'

'And did you phone her?'

'I decided to wait, but then the story was all over the papers. Your client Wetherby had shut her mouth forever.'

'Did you see her maid? A woman called Anna McKinnan.'

'I suppose so. There was a woman who showed me in and said goodbye to me when I left.'

'Did you tell her what you'd asked Ludmilla?'

'No. I simply said we'd had a nice chat. It's no good you asking me these questions, Mr Rumpole. You're going to get a blast from the *Fortress*. "Barristers who get fat and rich on defending hopeless cases", that kind of thing.'

'I resent that,' I told him.

'I'm sure you do. I'm just warning you what to expect.'

'I may be fat, but I'm certainly not rich.'

So he left me, and I poured out the remainder of the bottle. I thought of Lars, and then of Lars Porsena of Clusium, who, in the old poem,

> ... bade his messengers ride forth,
> East and west and south and north,
> To summon his array.

This Lars's 'messenger' would go forth in every issue of the *Daily Fortress* to portray Rumpole as the man who throws public money away on non-existent defences.

And then I remembered a possibly valuable piece of evidence that Lars had brought to me, so I raised a glass to him in spite of everything, an absent friend.

16

'What time did you phone Flyte Street?'

'About a quarter past twelve.'

'You weren't in the phone box?'

'No. I'd already copied down her number. I made sure no one could hear me.'

'So what time did you get to the flat?'

'Just before one.'

'And you've told us about your conversation with the maid, Anna McKinnan. Did she tell you anything else you can remember?'

'She said they hadn't had many customers so I could go straight in.'

'Nothing else?'

'She said she hoped I wasn't a bloody journalist.'

I felt a small thrill of pleasure. The god who looks after defending barristers was giving me a little bit of his help.

'What time was it when you went into the bedroom and found Ludmilla dead?'

'About one thirty. I was getting worried about being late back to work. Then the maid locked me in.'

'And then the police arrived at about two thirty with a police doctor?'

'I suppose so. I was arrested and taken down to the car before they examined the body.' There was a silence and then my client looked at me and said quietly, 'It's hopeless, isn't it?'

'Not entirely.'

'You think you're going to work some bloody miracle?'

'It has been known!'

'If you were a miracle worker they'd've given it to you before now, wouldn't they?'

'Given me what?'

'The QC. You haven't got it, have you?'

'Not as yet.'

'It's so humiliating. Everyone I meet at exercise. All those on serious charges like murder or rape or whatever. They've all got QCs to defend them.'

'Have they ever been defended by me, these people?'

'I don't believe so.'

'I thought as much. If they had been they probably wouldn't be in a prison exercise yard. Anyway, a distinguished High Court judge, Leonard Bullingham, is backing my application.'

'We live in hope then?'

'Yes,' I told him. 'That's the best way for us both to live.'

'I don't know why you wanted to see him again, Mr Rumpole. Every time we go down there it seems clearer that he's got no defence. I'm afraid he's wasting our time.'

'Not mine, certainly.' I had a disconsolate solicitor on my hands as we sought the comfort of Pommeroy's on our return to the Temple. '"Never plead guilty," that's my motto. You heard what Ackerman told us about the time of death?'

'You think that's going to get him off?'

'Not in itself perhaps, although it might be

enough before an intelligent jury. To be sure, we need to find out a lot more about Ludmilla. If our client didn't kill her, who did? And why?'

'We haven't got an answer to the question.'

'She was meant to report regularly to a police station in the Paddington area. Did she?'

'I did ask. They've got no record of her reporting anywhere in Paddington.'

'I thought not. So what would have happened if she hadn't been discovered at Dover?'

'She'd have gone on to a garage in some office block in the Canary Wharf area. Didn't Scottie Thompson tell us that?'

'Exactly. As I would expect, you have the facts of the case at your fingertips. But which garage, under precisely which office block?'

'I have no idea.'

'There may be stories going around. There can't be many office blocks where girls get out of boxes. We need a detective. You can put it down to further inquiries. Send for Fig Newton.'

Ferdinand Ian Gilmour Newton, clothed in the old mac he wore in all weathers, and with the cold that apparently afflicted him in all weathers, was just the man to pick up any rumours that might be going round about girls in boxes in the Canary Wharf area.

17

Shortly after these events I received an invitation from the corridors of power. Henry rang to say in a voice full of awe and wonder that the office of the Minister for Constitutional Affairs had rung. It seemed the Minister would like to share a drink with Mr Rumpole in his club.

It was not until then that I remembered who the Minister for Constitutional Affairs was. He was none other than the Peter Plaistow, QC, MP, who had dangled the offer of a Circuit (I call them Circus) Judgeship to me during the case in which he was prosecuting the unfortunate Dr Khan, who was accused of terrorism, a case which I won, if you remember, satisfactorily alone and without a leader.

So there we were, under the soft lights of the Sheridan Club, where drinks were asked for quietly and members and their friends murmured together, so the occasional loud welcome or braying laugh seemed as out of place as it would in a chapel of rest.

Peter Plaistow looked aged by his time in government. His boyish charm had faded, to be replaced by what I could only call a look of grim determination. His eyes seemed tired and his eyelids swollen, but he nonetheless greeted me with enthusiasm and ordered champagne for both of us.

When we were seated with our drinks and he had told me how pleased he was to see me, he said, 'I see Leonard Bullingham is backing your application for silk. I thought you two were sworn enemies. How did you manage that?'

'I think my wife managed it.'

'The remarkable Hilda? Well done her! Of course you have to go through a lot of tedious stuff before the new committee, but in the end the decision will come to me as Minister for Constitutional Affairs.'

What was I meant to do precisely? Offer to buy the next round of drinks? Thank him profusely? I hadn't thought that the process of sliding into a silk gown could be managed so easily. But then I was to discover the real purpose of our meeting in the Sheridan Club.

'Immigration!' The Minister for Constitutional Affairs almost spat out the word, as though it were some sort of incurable disease. 'The curse of all governments.'

'Is it as bad as that?'

'Worse. They imagine we are letting in floods of foreigners who'll take away their jobs, their houses, certainly their wives, probably their children if they get half a chance. And when it comes to letting in Russian prostitutes ... I can just imagine the headlines in the *Fortress*.' He had obviously been following my little Flyte Street murder case.

'Someone decided to set the girl free to apply for permanent residence.'

'We heard you'd been making inquiries.'

There was a pause then while the Minister for Constitutional Affairs sipped thoughtfully at his champagne, then he said, 'Of course that was all long before the murder. How or why she got into the country can't be any part of your defence.'

'I'm not entirely sure of that.'

'Well, it's obvious, isn't it?'

'There's a lot in this case which isn't entirely obvious.'

At this the Minister drained his glass and gave me a smile which I felt unusually chilly. 'I hope your application for silk goes well, Rumpole,' he said. 'I can't be sure what view the committee'll take of you. They haven't had many barristers who've been given an ASBO by the members of their own chambers. We'll have to see how that works out.' He looked at his watch. 'I've got to rush. Dinner at the Swedish Embassy. That'll hardly be a laugh a minute.'

Then he left me to think back on our conversation, which I hadn't found particularly amusing either.

18

WELL-KNOWN CRIMINAL BARRISTER
FACES JAIL FOR BREAK OF ASBO!

Mr Horace Rumpole, famous for his defence tactics in
some high-profile murder cases, is having to defend a
new client in the magistrates' court today – himself!

The news was blasted to its readers by the *Daily
Fortress*. And now I found myself what I had never
thought to be, a defendant before a 'district judge'
(stipendiary magistrates we used to call them), rising

to make a final speech on behalf of that dangerous and determined criminal Horace Rumpole, BA (the letters added after a rather poor study of the law at Keble College).

Of course I had not taken the ASBO seriously. Who could have? I kept a bottle or two of Pommeroy's Very Ordinary in the filing cabinet and I lit up my small cigars without noticing any rise in the water level along the Thames Embankment.

I did notice an embarrassed silence when I entered the client's room. Mizz Liz Probert seemed too embarrassed to speak to me as I picked up some documents concerning my ASBO and filed them in the wastepaper basket, unread. But when I asked our clerk, Henry, if I was in court next week, he told me that I was, in order to attend my own trial.

The prosecution was undertaken by a certain Lesley Perkins, a lady counsel who had to be corrected by me several times during her opening address. I had not even been paid the compliment of a competent prosecutor. No one from my chambers had the time to turn up at the proceedings. The press benches, however, were full of excited scribblers eager to join in the persecution of the Lion of the Old Bailey.

What surprised me more was that Hilda had been particularly sympathetic as I left at breakfast time to face my final humiliation. She knew there were those in my chambers who were hellbent on destroying my reputation. 'They won't win, Rumpole,' she said as we parted and after she had cooked me a couple of eggs on a fried slice to give me strength for the fight to come. 'We'll get you out of this somehow,' she went on, in what I then thought was a vain promise, intended only to raise false hopes.

I had helpfully admitted the truth of all the complaints brought before the court. Now the district judge, a pale figure with a long, inquisitive nose who had clearly enjoyed my prosecution more than his normal trade of drink-driving and soliciting in the streets, said, 'Well, Mr Rumpole, what have you got to say for yourself?'

'I don't speak for myself, sir. I speak for all those unfortunate enough to be caught up in this new type of illegal procedure.'

'Are you calling the ASBO rules "illegal"? You'd better go back to Parliament and tell them they made a mistake.'

This unhappy attempt at a joke by the judge was aimed at the journalists, who rewarded it with suppressed titters.

'No need for that,' I told him. 'But you must see the absurdity of this nonsensical and inept piece of legislation. What is my crime? I have looked through the statutes over and over again and nowhere do I find that eating at your desk is a criminal activity.

'I keep a bottle or two of Pommeroy's Very Ordinary claret in my filing cabinet drawer. This is not Pichon-Longueville perhaps, but drinking it if you have the courage and the stamina is surely not a criminal offence.

'We live in an unhappy period when the government wants to use its legislative powers to tell us how to lead our lives. It wants to tell us what to eat and drink, what to smoke and how we cross the road. Children are not allowed to grow fat and if they do they are snatched from their families and put into a home. If you smoke cigarettes, you won't be treated by the doctor.

'There are plans afoot to turn us into a nation of vegans who drink carrot juice and go on hiking tours to the Lake District. This case is an object lesson in this form of tyranny. It's geared to send a man to prison for eating a slice of pie.

'In the great days of our history, magistrates such as you, sir, stood up against a tyrannical king who tried to enforce taxes not approved by Parliament.

'Today you're being asked to enforce laws against activities which have never been made crimes by our Parliament.

'You have your chance today, sir, to reject these illegal and inappropriate proceedings. You can stand up for justice. You have a chance today, sir, to become the Pym or Hampden of the City Magistrates' Court. You may be criticized by the thinking bureaucrats of Westminster, but you'll be acclaimed by all those who cherish our ancient freedoms, our constitution and the proper rule of law.'

I then sat down and saw the lonely figure on the bench look, I thought a little desperately, at the clock, from which he seemed to get some encouragement. 'I'm looking at the time,' he told us unnecessarily. 'I'll give my decision at two o'clock.'

'It's not too bad,' I told Bonny Bernard, who had acted as my solicitor for the case. 'I always wanted to know how it felt to appear in the dock, like my clients.'

'We must keep hoping for the best,' Bonny Bernard said without any particular conviction. 'We must always go on hoping.'

'I don't think "Sir" wants to be a John Hampden of the City. When I go down I'll get plenty of time for reading. I could read Milton. I've never really got on with him. Not many jokes in *Paradise Lost*, are there? Not too many laughs. Anyway, it'll be interesting to find out what life's like for your clients after you've lost their cases.'

But when we were called back to court I wasn't to be given the great opportunity of laughing away with Milton. I saw that Soapy Sam Ballard was in court, sitting beside the lady prosecutor, and as soon as 'Sir' was back in his seat she rose to say that my Head of Chambers, none other than the eminent Samuel Ballard, QC, had decided not to go on further with this case. He was anxious that any custodial sentence might prevent Mr Rumpole from practising, at least for a while, and he didn't think it was in the interests of his chambers, or the Bar in general, to proceed with a judgement against Rumpole.

Thus Rumpole was dismissed, with few words given.

What happened when we got back to court had been quite unexpected and so the shades of the prison-house vanished as 'Sir' reluctantly agreed.

*

'It must have been my final speech that did it,' I told Hilda when I got home that afternoon. 'That must have made them come to their senses.'

'It wasn't your final speech at all, Rumpole. It was all down to Leonard.'

'Leonard Bullingham?'

'Of course. He knows I want you to get your silk so I can pick up some of your future briefs. So he was going to ask your Head of Chambers not to go on with the case.'

'Did he?'

'He was away on circuit. I phoned to tell him that the case was on and he got hold of Sam Ballard in the lunchtime break. Apparently he told your Head of Chambers that he wouldn't be considered for a judgeship if he dragged his chambers' name through the courts.'

'Soapy Sam Ballard's being considered for a judgeship?'

'I told you that, Rumpole.'

'And your friend Leonard decided to help *me*?'

'He did it for *me*, Rumpole.'

'I'm sure he did.'

So fortune brings its mysterious changes. I was entering my future years at the Bar by courtesy of the Mad Bull, to whom I must be particularly grateful.

19

'You set me impossible tasks, Mr Rumpole.'

'Never mind. The impossible ones are often the easiest. They bring out the best in you. What've you got to report?'

I was sharing a portion of Melton Mowbray pie at my desk with Fig Newton, the ingenious and reliable detective who seemed to suffer from a perpetual cold. Free from the ASBO, we ate lunch and drank Château Thames Embankment from tumblers at my desk.

'It's taken me a time, Mr Rumpole. But I think I might be on to something.'

'I'm sure you are.'

'I had a drink in a number of bars and public houses round the Canary Wharf area.'

'Hard work for you.'

'It was a long time before I got a bit of news.'

'What sort of news?'

'Someone was talking about an empty bit of an office block in Tinkers Passage with a drive-in garage. Someone said they had heard the chattering of girls. Another said they had seen girls being driven away in a car. Foreign girls was what they reckoned.'

'God bless you, Fig! You're a detective without equal. So did you carry on your observation in this Tinkers Passage?'

'Several nights, but nothing happened.'

'Keep an eye on it. Oh, and see if you can find out who owns the building. That would be extremely helpful.'

Not long after the detective had left me there was a sharp tap on the door and it opened to admit Soapy Sam Ballard, the man whose accusations had landed Rumpole particularly close to the cooker.

'Well now, Rumpole.' Our Head of Chambers looked suitably embarrassed. 'I see you're enjoying your lunch.'

'No thanks to you, Ballard.' I didn't mince my words. 'If you'd had your way I'd be enjoying it under lock and key.'

'It wasn't my doing, Rumpole,' Soapy Sam protested. 'It was just that everyone else in Chambers felt that I had to take some steps to see that the views of the majority were respected.'

'The test of democracy is the tolerance shown by the majority to minority opinions. Didn't darling John Stuart Mill say something like that?'

'Mill?' Ballard looked puzzled. I hoped he might ask me what chambers this person was in.

'He thought you might be tolerant of people who fancy a slice of pie at their desk occasionally,' I said.

Ballard changed the subject. 'Is Mr Justice Bullingham a good friend of yours?'

'We are extremely close. He met my wife at her bridge club and now we are just one big happy family.'

'I acted quickly when he asked us to drop the case against you.'

'I noticed that.'

'And Bullingham is one of the judges who has the ear of the Minister for Constitutional Affairs?'

'Constantly. He has his ear night and day. Particularly when the time comes to appoint new judges.'

Soapy Sam's smile broadened. It became hopeful. 'Well,' he said, 'I'd best be getting along. A silk gown would suit you very well. Enjoy your lunch, Rumpole.'

The committee for the appointment of Queen's Counsel for England and Wales gathered itself together in a large room in the Outer Temple. Taking my place in front of this august assembly, I felt more nervous than I ever did before the most ferocious Old Bailey judge or even when I was the prisoner at the bar in the matter of the Rumpole ASBO. I was afraid of disappointing both Hilda and the accused murderer Graham Wetherby, and also of being robbed of a prize which I felt I so richly deserved.

The room, I thought as I took my seat, seemed to be full of people whom I had never seen in any court and who might not be able to tell a QC from a plastic surgeon. There was also a smattering of solicitors unknown to me and a few QCs who, having acquired silk gowns, might enjoy the sight of an elderly junior trying hard to climb up beside them.

In the chair was Dame Mildred Wrightsworth, a judge from the Family Division who specialized in sensational divorce cases and disputes over the custody of children.

'We've all seen your CV, Mr Rumpole.' The Dame spoke. 'It seems your practice is entirely criminal.'

'As I would wish it to be,' I told the meeting.

'Why do you say that?' came from one of the unknown QCs.

'Because if you go down to the Old Bailey you'll find that all life is there, the real world with all its sins, mistakes and occasional beauty and good behaviour. Go and watch the huge international companies suing each other in the Queen's Bench Division and you move into a world of fantasy and make-believe.'

'We have learned,' said another of the seated QCs, looking at me with disapproval, 'that you can be discourteous to judges.'

'Only when they act as leading counsel for the prosecution. Only when they indulge in such tricks as responding to the defence evidence with a sigh of disbelief. Only when they jump down from the bench and fight in the arena for a conviction. Then I feel they deserve a touch of discourtesy. Otherwise some of my very best friends are judges.'

'Really?' Dame Mildred looked sceptical. 'Which judges are these?'

'Well, a number of judges.'

'Such as?'

'Leonard Bullingham.' It was about time, I thought, that the Mad Bull gave me a little help. 'He's a family friend.'

'Indeed!' The Dame appeared to be softening. 'And he has written a letter in support of your application.'

'There you are,' I said. 'Apparent enemies in court but close friends out of it.' I cringed internally at the hypocrisy of the remark, but then decided that it was hypocrisy in a good cause.

'Speaking as one who has indulged in what you call the fantasy of company law from time to time, I'd like to ask you some questions about your attitude to crime.' This came from Stephen Barnes, QC, whose long neck and disdainful expression made him look, I often thought, like a particularly unfriendly camel. One day, long ago, before he ascended into the higher world of company lawyers, he had prosecuted me unsuccessfully. 'I believe you mostly defend.' He made this statement sound like an accusation.

'Always. I don't like the idea of cross-examining people into chokey.'

'Very well. Then I'd like to tell you what one of your own supporters said about you. We don't usually let applicants know what their supporters have said about them. But in this case the Chair has said I may do so. Is that right, Chair?'

'Quite right, Barnes,' the article of furniture agreed.

'The supporter in question,' Barnes continued, 'was a Mr Dennis Timson. You know him well?'

'Over the years, extremely well.'

'And might he be described as a habitual criminal?'

'Just as I might be described as a habitual defender.'

'He said you were an excellent brief.'

'That was kind of him.'

'And it didn't matter if he was innocent or guilty, you'd do a good job either way. Is that true?'

'Of course.'

'So you defend people you know to be guilty?'

'I don't know. It's not my business to decide that.

That's for the judge and jury. But if Mr Timson, or anyone else, tells me a story that's consistent with his innocence, it's my duty to defend him.'

'Even if you don't believe it?'

'I suspend my disbelief. My disbelief has been left hanging up in the robing room for years. My job is to put my client's case as well as it could be put. The prosecutor does the same and then the jury chooses to believe one of us. It's called our judicial system. It seems to work more fairly than any other form of criminal trial, if you want my opinion.'

'So it means that you have appeared for some pretty terrible people?'

'The more terrible they are, the more they need defending.'

'So morality doesn't enter into it?'

'Yes, it does. The morality of making our great system of justice work. Of protecting the presumption of innocence.'

'So you never judge your clients?'

'Of course not. I told you, judging isn't my job. I'm like a doctor – people come to me in trouble and I'm here to get them out of it as painlessly as possible. And it would be a peculiar sort of doctor who only cured healthy people.'

There was a silence. Barnes seemed to have run out of ammunition. Then Madam Chair spoke. 'Mr Rumpole, you have defended yourself expertly.'

'I wasn't defending myself,' I told her. 'I was defending the British constitution.'

'That too, of course. Speaking entirely for myself, I was impressed by your argument, and you have important backing from Mr Justice Bullingham.'

'My family friend.'

'Of course. But, as you realize, the final decision rests with the Minister for Constitutional Affairs.'

'It's been a pleasure.'

It certainly had. In spite of Barnes's cross-examination, the faces round the table had produced a few nods and smiles. Had I actually won a case? I told myself that it was about time I had a bit of luck and, after all, I deserved it.

20

After my appearance before the QC committee life for Rumpole took on a slightly superior turn. I had reasonable hopes that Madam Chair would recommend me for a silk gown and this would satisfy the needs of my wife, Hilda, my murder suspect, Graham Wetherby, and, I have to admit it, myself. At odd lonely moments, I would repeat the rolling phrase 'Horace Rumpole, one of Her Majesty's counsel learned in the law'. In my wildest imaginings I thought that the Queen, faced with one of the many difficulties in life, might send for Rumpole for assistance.

One evening when I came home I found the flat in Froxbury Mansions unusually spick and span. There were fresh flowers in vases in the sitting room and our kitchen table was spread with a bright cloth, shining candles and polished glasses. It was laid, I couldn't help noticing, for three people. I asked She Who Must if we were expecting company.

'Leonard invited himself, as it so happened. So you'd better tidy yourself up. I don't think you should be having dinner in one of those awful sweaters.'

'Is it white tie and tails?'

'Don't be ridiculous. Just your nice tweed jacket, not the one you burned a hole in.'

'That was an accident with a small cigar.'

'It doesn't matter how it happened. Just put on the other one.'

So I changed out of the regulation black jacket and striped trousers into more relaxed evening wear, although I doubted that dinner with the Mad Bull chez Rumpole would be, in any sense, a relaxed affair. But when he arrived, promptly, the Bull was wreathed in smiles, casually dressed in a jacket quite without cigar holes and corduroy trousers.

'I spurned the Bankers' Annual Guest Night for the chance of a relaxed dinner with the two of you,' he told us.

Hearing him say this made me feel vaguely guilty, as though we should have put on some sort of entertainment to compensate for his missing the Bankers' annual do.

'That was so sweet of you, Leonard,' Hilda said. 'Wasn't that sweet of him, Rumpole?'

'Amazingly so.'

'Well, go on then – offer Leonard a drink.'

'I'm afraid it's only Pommeroy's Very Ordinary,' I said when I was opening the bottle. 'You might have had decent bottles at the Bankers'.'

'Perhaps. But I wouldn't have had the company of Hilda then, would I?' At this my wife gave the Bull a small satisfied smile, until he added, 'And you too of course, Rumpole.'

We had polished off the beef stew and were on to the baked jam roll when she reminded me to thank the Bull for all the support he'd given me.

'Of course. You saved me from chokey over the anti-social behaviour order.'

'And backed your claim for silk,' Hilda added.

'Yes, of course. Thank you for that. I think I ended up with the committee on my side.'

'Think nothing of it, Rumpole. I know that Hilda didn't want a husband behind bars. And I knew she'd prefer one with a silk gown on his back.'

'Horace Rumpole, QC,' Hilda ran her tongue round the words, 'that's how they'll paint your name up on the chambers' door.'

'Isn't it a bit too soon for that? The Minister for Constitutional Affairs has to approve –'

'That'll be a formality.' I noticed that the Bull was answering Hilda and not me.

'So will you say thank you, Rumpole?'

'Yes, of course.'

After that we ate in silence for a while, with Hilda making sure that the Bull's plate was well supplied and that I paid him a further tribute.

'I've got even more reasons to be grateful to you, Judge.'

'Please call me Leonard.'

'All right then, Leonard. Those arguments we had in court.'

'Your husband *is* very argumentative, Hilda.'

'Don't I know it.'

'Whenever you failed to remind the jury of part of the defence, or stepped down into the arena to cross-examine one of my witnesses, it clarified my understanding of how justice ought to be done.'

There was silence. Then the Bull smiled and said, 'You're joking, of course.'

'Yes, of course.'

'Rumpole is always joking,' Hilda explained. 'It really does him no good at all.'

That night I left Hilda and the judge sitting in front of the gas fire and never at a loss for words. The last thing I heard, as I went early to bed, was my wife offering our guest a hot drink. It had taken someone with the strength of character and dominant personality of She Who Must Be Obeyed to tame the wild Bull at long last.

2 1

After these somewhat dramatic events – my hair's-breadth escape from chokey, my apparent success with the QC committee and my reception of the Mad Bull in the matrimonial home – life seemed to drift on much as usual, that is to say, I got enough work to keep the bailiffs from the door. But none of the cases I was doing then – apart from the Flyte Street murder, of course – were interesting or unusual enough to win a place in these chronicles.

Then one morning, when Bonny Bernard and

I were having coffee in the Old Bailey canteen — waiting for the jury to come back after a particularly boring breaking and entering — Bernard gave me a piece of information that was to open a door to some far more serious goings-on.

'It's your Peter Timson,' Bernard told me. 'He's broken his ASBO.'

'What did he do, remind me.'

'Kicked a football into the street next to his. The street with all the posh people in. His dad wants you to appear for him again. Do you really want to do it?'

'What did my darling old sheep of the Lake District say? We come into the world trailing clouds of glory and then terrible things begin to happen. "Shades of the prison-house begin to close upon the growing Boy".'

Back in my chambers I was still contemplating the fate of young Peter Timson when there was a knock on the door and Mizz Liz Probert entered into the presence, apparently unashamed.

'Rumpole!' she greeted me. 'I'm so glad you're back.'

'Are you really, Mizz Liz? You did your best to have me put away.'

'Oh, I never wanted that. I thought that they'd just tick you off a bit for breaking your ASBO. I never thought for a moment about prison.'

'Don't worry. It might have been quite interesting.'

'And Claude said it was something we had to do. To make Chambers more eco-friendly.'

'Has he noticed that the Sahara Desert has moved to Spain since I lit my last cigar?'

'He does take such things seriously, Rumpole, and he's a wonderful man.'

I thought of many adjectives I could apply to Claude, but wonderful wasn't one of them.

'And he's not happy, I'm sure you know that. His wife doesn't really understand him. Has he told you that?'

'No. But I bet he told you.'

Her Honour Dame Justice Phillida Erskine-Brown – once Phillida Trant and the Portia of our chambers – had married Claude in what I thought was a moment of weakness. 'Perhaps she doesn't think there's much to understand,' was what I didn't say.

'He can't talk to her,' Mizz Liz told me, 'like he can talk to me.'

'So what does he talk to you about?'

'How he feels passed over and he'll never be a judge since his wife's got it. And he knows they don't give him the most important cases because he's a judge's husband.'

'Or is it because he's a lousy cross-examiner?' was, again, something I didn't say.

'So we've become really friendly.'

'I thought you never liked the chap.'

'But it's different now. I sometimes feel that I'm not getting the sort of work I deserve and he understands that. So when he said you should be made to take the ASBO seriously, I agreed. I never thought of prison.'

'I've told you, Mizz Liz, dismiss it from your mind. Devote your time to understanding Claude.' And I didn't add, 'It shouldn't take you very long.'

'And he's going to take me to the opera next week. Do you go to the opera, Rumpole?'

'Hardly at all.' And I remembered an old saying: 'If a thing's too silly to say, then sing it.'

'I have wheels, Mr Rumpole. To be used in important cases and cases of difficulty, as this one is,' Fig Newton said proudly. 'But you must have wheels that sink into the background. My old Golf is just such a vehicle.'

The information Fig had obtained was, it appeared, too confidential to be revealed in Pommeroy's, so Bonny Bernard and I met with the tireless sleuth in my room in Chambers.

He had parked and then watched the lock-up garage under the office block in the Canary Wharf area for several nights. On the fourth night he struck lucky.

'I was keeping observation from a side street just opposite when I was rewarded by the arrival of a lorry just after midnight. The garage door was left open and some men were there who helped the lorry driver unload packing cases, which were moved into the garage.'

After the garage doors were closed, Fig thought he heard male and female voices. He kept observation until four a.m., when a large van-like car, which Fig described as a 'people carrier', arrived. Three girls emerged from the garage and were helped into the vehicle.

Fig was able to follow them to a house in Battersea, into which one of the girls was taken. Then the people carrier drove on to an address in Clapham. An escort rang on the bell of the house in question, where the door was opened by a middle-aged woman who took the other two girls inside. Although Fig tried to follow the people carrier further, he was delayed at some traffic lights and lost contact with it.

The industrious Fig had also been to the land registry and discovered that the empty block and garages were owned by a company called Helsing. After further inquiries he tried to ring Helsing but found that they were not answering their phone.

Then I asked Fig for the address of the house in Clapham where the girl was deposited. When he told me I laughed so loudly that I was in danger of getting another ASBO.

22

'Have you got it?'

The question was fired at me as soon as Graham Wetherby was delivered to the interview room in Brixton Prison.

'Got what exactly?'

'The QC.' Wetherby appeared to be more anxious about my promotion than about the state of his defence.

'Not quite yet,' I told him. 'But I have been before the selection committee and they as good as told me it was in the bag. The thing has to be rubber-stamped by the Minister for Constitutional Affairs.'

'So you'll be QC at my trial?'

'I'll do my very best.'

'Mr Rumpole,' Bonny Bernard came to my rescue, 'will give you considerable service whether he's a QC or not.'

'The most important thing,' I told my client, 'is to remember the times. We worked them out the last time I was here. Twelve fifteen you made a telephone call from the office. And you arrived at the flat in Flyte Street at . . .'

'Around one pm.'

'That's right, and you got into the room at . . .'

'One thirty.'

'Excellent! And the police and the police doctor were there at two thirty. That's when the doctor examined the body.'

I had agreed to this conference to keep Graham Wetherby feeling properly looked after, not because I thought we had anything more helpful to discuss. I looked at my watch; there was still almost half an hour before we could decently leave. What could we discuss? The weather, ASBOs, the iniquities of a government that tried to tell us how to be good and true? None of these topics seemed suitable, so I played for safety. 'Tell me a little more about yourself. I know you work in the Home Office. What sort of job do you do exactly?'

'Extra office accommodation for property and human resources without our Queen Anne's Gate headquarters. It has to do with positioning.'

'I'm sure it has, but could you just translate a little?'

'The Home Office has grown so big we have to find external office accommodation for human resources.'

'Does that mean people?'

'Of course it does.' Wetherby looked at me as though I was a child who had not quite come to grips with the alphabet. And I thought that my client's job was probably so dull and uneventful that an occasional visit to such places as the Flyte Street flat might have become a necessity.

'You dealt with property companies – I mean, when your office was expanding?'

'A lot of them.'

'Does the name Helsing mean anything to you?'

I thought it was just worth trying. Graham Wetherby considered, and shook his head.

'I'm afraid not.'

'It doesn't matter.' I had nothing more to

ask, but Wetherby, afraid of the loneliness of his cell, looked at me, begging me to stay, so we went on talking about nothing very much until the warden came in and told us our interview time was up. As we left my client was still worrying, asking if I'd do my best to become a QC in time for his trial.

And then I was back to where this story began, in the South London Magistrates' Court with young Peter Timson, who stood, as I had done, within the shades of the prison-house for breaking the terms of an ASBO.

'You'll do your best for him, won't you, Mr Rumpole?' Bertie Timson seemed suddenly worried. If he wanted his son to follow in his footsteps, he obviously didn't want it quite yet. 'The lad's too young for prison. In a year or two perhaps, he'll know how to deal with it. But now he's far too young.'

'Don't you worry,' I told him, as though I had complete confidence in young Peter's defence.

We were in the entrance hall of the magistrates' court, together with the casual streetwalkers and angry businessmen hauled up for drink-driving. I was with Bonny Bernard and Fig Newton, who had come reluctantly to court, where I thought he might be needed.

Then I saw Parkes, the solicitor employed by the council for the prosecution of such dangerous villains as young Peter Timson. With him was a tall woman, perhaps in her late fifties, with bright hair piled high on her head, a long neck disappearing into a fur-collared leather jacket and an extremely discontented expression. I looked at Fig, who nodded. Then Parkes approached me.

'I've got Mrs Englefield to come.'

'I know. We served a witness summons on her.'

'She's a very busy woman.'

'So I understand.'

'I shall tell the magistrate her evidence is quite unnecessary. I'm not going to call her.'

'Then I'll call her as part of my defence.'

Parkes looked at me with extreme suspicion.

'What are you up to, Rumpole?' was what he said.

All I could answer was, 'Wait and see.'

The court was no better or worse than it had been before. The same Madam Chair sat between the same two bookends, the plump fellow with the Trade Union badge and the thin schoolmaster. The same obedient usher called 'Timson. Application

to enforce anti-social behaviour order. The defendant is here.'

And I turned my head to see the diminutive
figure of Peter Timson in what passed as a dock in
the South London Magistrates' Court.

'Mr Rumpole is here for the defendant Timson.'

'Let's call him Peter,' I said as I rose to my feet.

'Why?' Madam Chair seemed unlikely to agree.
'We remember you from when this case was before
us earlier and we made the order, Mr Rumpole, in
spite of your lengthy speech. We hope you won't
feel inclined to mention Nelson Mandela in this
court again.'

'If you wish it.' I gave her what I knew was an
insincere smile of obedience. 'Nelson Mandela shall
be left out of these proceedings entirely.'

'I'm glad to hear it.'

'I merely ask that my client should be referred
to as Peter as he is a twelve-year-old child.'

'We are all aware of that, Mr Rumpole.'

'So you should be. And is a child able to be sent
to prison?'

'To a young offenders' institution, Mr Rumpole.'

'Call it what you like, it's a prison where he can
be taught to do more crime and come out a threat
to society.'

Madam Chair then conferred with her bookends and came back with, 'Very well. We'll call him Peter if you like. But it won't make the slightest difference to the proceedings.'

'I'm much obliged.'

I was about to sit down, but after a bit of advice from the clerk to Madam Chair she said, 'Mr Rumpole, do we understand that your client admits the breaking of the order?'

'I'm not admitting anything until we've heard it properly passed in court.'

'We have read Mrs Englefield's statement.'

'That's the point. It was a statement by a witness who didn't offer herself for cross-examination. That's not evidence at all. Hopefully, this Mrs Englefield is in court.'

'Because you took out a witness summons,' Parkes told the magistrates helpfully.

'Exactly so. I did that so I can cross-examine her after she's taken the oath and then we might come to the truth.'

'The truth about your client's footballing?'

'And a few related matters.'

At this Madam Chair seemed at a loss and sought the advice of her clerk, who stood up from below her. After she had enjoyed a prolonged earful, she asked, 'What is your authority, Mr Rumpole, for saying that a statement has to be proved by a witness on oath and available for cross-examination?'

'No written authority at present. Although I gather that directions are to be given shortly.'

'Directions? By whom exactly?'

'The Minister for Constitutional Affairs.'

'In what case?'

'No case. But I know he finds it outrageous that a young child should be deprived of his liberty on charges that have never been tested by cross-examination.'

The atmosphere in court changed rapidly. Madam Chair muttered some urgent remarks to the bookends, then she said, 'Mr Parkes, I don't suppose you'd object to putting Mrs Englefield in the witness box so that Mr Rumpole might ask her a few questions? It seems a fairly simple issue, but we have to take into account the view of the Minister for Constitutional Affairs.'

'No, Madam. I have no objection, if you have the time.'

'I'm afraid we do.' Madam Chair spoke for the bookends too. 'We can only hope that Mr Rumpole will keep it short.'

So the witness entered the box, swore on the Bible and gave her name as Mrs Harriet Englefield and her address as 15 Beechwood Grove. She swore that since the first order was made she had seen young Peter Timson, the boy in the dock, on at least six occasions enter her quiet and secluded street in search of a football which had strayed from its proper place in Rampton Road.

When Parkes sat down Madam Chair gave me a look of exasperation and said, 'You may put your questions shortly, Mr Rumpole.'

'I hope to keep them short, Madam. That depends on the witness.'

'So how can I help you, Mr Rumpole?' Mrs Englefield gave me a tolerant smile.

'Quite easily, I hope. Perhaps you could tell us why you didn't want this little footballer hanging around your street.'

'It disturbed me.'

'Not much of a disturbance, was it? A small boy entering your road for a few minutes to retrieve a football.'

'You don't understand, Mr Rumpole. We buy our houses in the Grove for peace and quiet. There are important people living there, doctors and a retired general who is writing a book. Then there is my aged mother, who lives with me. They all need tranquillity. And of course I need it for my work. I have a good many patients. They come to me for treatment.'

'And what sort of treatment do you give them?'

'I give spiritual healing. We sit together and think of our own spaces. Then they like to talk. They may have troubled auras and I do my best to cleanse the space around them.'

'And what are their troubles exactly?'

'Unhappy marriages or affairs. Feelings of use-lessness when they have lost touch with the life force. Feelings of doubt and insecurity.'

'And I suppose,' Madam Chair was out to help the witness, 'you need peace and quiet for that?'

'Absolutely. I chose Beechwood Grove because it *was* so quiet.'

There was a silent moment during which I considered my best form of attack. Then Madam Chair clipped in with, 'Is that all you have to ask, Mr Rumpole?'

'Not quite all,' I told her, and turned my attention to the witness. Then I led off with, 'Mrs Englefield, no doubt you've heard of the importation of girls who pay good money to get smuggled in to the country and are set to work as prostitutes? Have you heard of that?'

'Yes.' The witness closed her eyes in an apparent effort to remember. 'I may have read something about it.'

'I have to suggest you know a great deal more about it than that.'

'I don't know what Mr Rumpole is suggesting.' This interruption came from the prosecutor.

'Then sit quietly and you'll find out.' I was beginning to lose patience with Parkes. 'Now, let me take you back to 10 May.'

'I can't remember what I was doing then.'

'Can't you? It was something rather sensational. Don't worry. I'm here to remind you. The night before, a number of girls from a distant country had been smuggled into England and left in a warehouse somewhere near Canary Wharf. They were to be distributed to various addresses to work as prostitutes.'

'Mr Rumpole! Is this really necessary?' It was Madam Chair who interrupted this time.

'Absolutely essential to my case. And when the Minister spoke of cross-examination he meant un-interrupted cross-examination.'

This appeared to quieten the tribunal enough for me to continue.

'That morning a witness I shall call saw the girls moved from the warehouse and distributed to certain addresses. At four forty-five a people carrier drove up to your house in Beechwood Grove. Two girls were delivered to you. My witness will identify you as the lady who opened the door to them and let them into your house. Are you really going to tell us that they came to you for spiritual healing?'

Mrs Englefield didn't answer, so I went on with my case.

'I have to suggest to you that the sole reason why you didn't want little boys kicking footballs round your house is that they might see too much! They might learn too much about you. They might tell stories of mysterious foreign girls who had been shipped over the Channel in the backs of lorries and delivered at your door in the early hours of the morning. Delivered to the Beechwood Grove brothel.'

The woman in the witness box stood silent, staring at me with a look of hatred. Then the industrious Parkes sprang into action. He said that these were serious allegations which had come out of the blue and that he would have to take further instructions. He asked for an adjournment to consider his position. To this suggestion Rumpole most generously agreed.

Bonny Bernard and I got back from the pub, replete with bangers, mash and Guinness, to be received by an anxious Parkes, who asked me to agree to a statement to be made by him in court. 'Mrs Englefield,' it said, 'denies any and all of the suggestions made to her about girls arriving at her house. However, on further consideration, she does not wish to send such a young boy into custody, so she intends to discontinue proceedings on the ASBO.'

'And never to reinstate them,' I suggested.

'All right, Mr Rumpole. She really has no choice.'

Bertie Timson told his son that I was a 'magnificent brief'. Peter and I shook hands and so, as a satisfied client, he left me.

It may not have been one of my greatest wins, but thanks to Fig Newton it was sorted out admirably. I was left wishing that all the problems of my life could be solved so satisfactorily.

23

It was at about this time, if my memory serves me rightly, that our chambers in Equity Court were invaded, not by terrorists, as Ballard had always feared, but by a youngish, that is to say around thirty-year-old, barrister by the name of Christopher Kidmoth.

'It is a significant honour for our chambers,' Ballard told me, 'to have the grandson of Lord Chancellor Quarant join us.'

I had read the speeches of the old Lord Chancellor in the House of Lords, including the one on consent to rape while drunk. In my view, old Quarant had made a bit of a pig's breakfast of the law at that time.

'After his pupillage they wouldn't give Christopher a place in his grandfather's old chambers. Things have changed, Rumpole. Family connections don't ensure you a place nowadays.'

'But you took him on here because of his family connections, didn't you?'

'Not at all, Rumpole. Perish the thought. I voted in favour of admitting him because he's a bright young barrister who might be able to fill a place made vacant by any one of us who wishes to retire.'

'Don't look at me, Ballard,' I warned Soapy Sam. 'You're not getting rid of me. I have no thought of retiring.'

'Not now, perhaps. But the day will come . . .'

'When I die with my wig on, that's true. Until then I'm staying with you.' I might have added, 'Because nothing they sling at me in court could be as bad as having to confront, every day and all day, the changing moods and the general disapproval of She Who Must Be Obeyed.'

'I still feel that the time may come,' Ballard said hopefully.

*

A few days later I saw a group that contained Mizz Liz, Claude Erskine-Brown, our clerk, Henry, and Hoskins. As I passed this apparently merry gathering on my way back to my room, after a short taking and driving away at Snaresbrook, a fair-haired youth, whom I took to be the new arrival, Kidmoth, called after me, 'There goes the oldest inhabitant! Are you off to your room for a picnic, Rumpole?'

I didn't demean myself by answering this sally. I might have said, 'I'm sorry that none of you seem to have any work to do!' But I passed silently through to my quarters.

Another week or two passed before I was made particularly aware of our newest member. A cold spring had turned into a warm June when he entered my room without knocking and settled himself comfortably into my client's chair. He flicked a falling blond lock back from his eyes.

I was working and lunching at my desk at the time and I didn't give him a particularly warm welcome.

'You know what this chambers lacks, Rumpole?' he started off with.

'Repairs to the upstairs loo? It flushes reluctantly.'

'No. Not that. Team spirit! Like we had in our house at Harrow. At the moment it's just a collection of individuals, all competing against each other.'

'I don't feel I'm competing against anybody.'

'You're a one-off, Rumpole. Everyone knows that.'

'I'm not sure I'd want to be anything else.'

'You will, Rumpole. You will. I'm going to invite everyone at 4 Equity Court to our annual herb garden barbecue at Quarant.'

'At where?'

'Quarant Castle. I know it sounds grand, but it's quite relaxed. And Ma and Pa will be thrilled to see you all. Everyone to bring wives and children, the whole shooting match. Oh, by the way, Sammy Ballard told me that Leonard Bullingham is a close personal friend of yours.'

I was silent for a moment, astonished at hearing our Head of Chambers called 'Sammy'. Then I said, 'He's a close personal friend of my wife.'

'Good! I'll ask him too. And Mrs Justice Erskine-Brown. You can't have too many judges.'

'I'm not sure I agree with that,' I told him.

Then he said he was off to take coffee with 'Sammy' Ballard, and he left the presence.

*

The invitation came a couple of weeks later.

*Lord and Lady Quarant invite Mr and Mrs Horace Rumpole
to their summer party in the herb garden. Dress informal.*

I tried to hide this dreaded message under my
breakfast plate, but Hilda spotted it immediately.

'The dear Quarants. Everyone says they're
utterly charming.'

'The son's in our chambers. Christopher
Kidmoth. He threatened something of the sort.'

'"Dress informal". That means a new summer
frock, Rumpole.'

At Kidmoth's suggestion a bus was hired to take
us all from the Temple to the herb garden party.
Informal dress was interpreted in many ways. Sam
Ballard had a straw hat and Claude Erskine-Brown
was tricked out in full cricket whites. I was struck
by the appearance of his wife. Phillida was once a
sparkling young beauty, appointed the unofficial
Portia of our chambers, but she had achieved a
middle-aged loveliness and a sort of authority that
made everyone make way for her.

Hilda had purchased a deep orange creation. The
Mad Bull, I thought inappropriately, appeared in

long khaki shorts, while Henry and the secretaries from the clerk's room were dressed as for a summer holiday in Ibiza. I had dug out a white cotton jacket, now yellowing with age, and Hoskins had brought a selection of his daughters, who huddled together and whispered to each other.

Surrounded by the suburban spread of south-east London, Quarant Castle rose like 'a good deed in a naughty world'.

We tramped across a drawbridge into a small courtyard and then found ourselves in a country garden which seemed to have sought refuge inside the sturdy walls. We passed roses, delphiniums and hollyhocks in bloom, and then we went into the herb garden, where thyme and rosemary and mint gently swayed in the breeze.

It was at the corner of this garden that a brazier was lit and Christopher Kidmoth put on an apron and a chef's hat and started to cook, while two servants from the castle handed round red wine in paper cups.

In the course of time, while I was trying to deal with a sausage in a bun, an elderly, grey-haired fellow bowled up beside me in a wheelchair.

'Singed meat!' he said. 'Do you really enjoy eating singed meat?'

'That seems to be the only thing there is.'

'It was all Christopher's idea. He loves having people to eat singed meat in the garden. By the way, he was telling me that you're one of the barristers, Rumpole. He says you're top hole at the job.'

'That has to be me,' I admitted.

'He says you can get people off in murder cases.'

'I have a certain reputation . . .'

'You can get them off, even if they did it?'

'No. Only if it can't be proved that they did it.'

'Ah. I see. Very clever!'

There was a pause and then the old fellow, whom I took to be Lord Quarant, looked round the assembled company. 'The trouble is,' he said, 'I feel I'd like to commit murder almost daily. Stubbs the gardener, who insists on planting vulgar-coloured dahlias. Mrs Donovan the cook, who won't do me a decent macaroni cheese.' Then he lowered his voice. 'My wife, who tells me that at my age I'm lucky not to be dead. If I do any of them in, would you defend me?'

'It would be a pleasure,' I said, to humour the old chap.

'It'd be a pleasure!' Lord Quarant threw back his head and shook with laughter. 'Would it really?'

Before I could answer he bowled himself off

to greet some new arrivals, neighbours perhaps, whom he might wish to kill.

By now Hilda was deep in conversation with Claude, and Mizz Liz was being chatted up by the heir to Quarant Castle. Having downed two or three paper cupfuls of red wine, which was only a shade less appealing than Pommeroy's Very Ordinary, I stepped through an archway in the hedge in the hope of finding a private place.

After relieving myself I walked on, seeking peace and quiet, between the hedges, until an extraordinary spectacle met my eyes.

In an embrasure in the hedge the Mad Bull was seated very close to Mrs Justice Erskine-Brown on a white painted iron seat. As he kissed her I saw his hand on her knee slide towards the opening of her fashionably short skirt. I beat a hasty retreat, and I didn't think that they had noticed me. But the vision of the two judges kissing had a lasting effect on me.

24

Extract from the Memoirs of Hilda Rumpole

Leonard Bullingham has taken a shine to Dame Phillida Erskine-Brown. I could tell by the way he gawped at her at Quarant Castle. Afterwards he kept telling me what a handsome woman she was. Well, she hasn't worn so badly, but of course, I told him, she's knocking on and their twins, Tristan and Isolde, must be quite grown up.

All the same, I said to him, I wish she could just relax and be her age. That streaky hair-do and ridiculously short skirt were quite unsuitable. All I could say about her appearance nowadays was 'mutton dressed as lamb'.

I did get a bit jealous though when he told me at the bridge club how very much Phillida had enjoyed lunch at the Sheridan. I couldn't help remembering how he had once taken me for lunch at his club.

And then there was the question of the flicks. I was particularly anxious to see the new *Pirates of the Caribbean* film as I am very taken with Johnny Depp. It was hopeless asking Rumpole to accompany me, but I remembered that Leonard had taken me to see a film in the days when he was, so to speak, courting me.

When I told him my idea about the flicks he actually said, quite calmly, 'I've fixed up to see that with Phillida.'

25

Events, which up till then had passed in a leisurely way since the days when I appeared in the ASBO scandal for Peter Timson, were now hurrying towards a climax, so that, as Hamlet's mother was fond of saying, they almost trod on each other's heels.

'You'll never guess what happened last night,' Mizz Liz Probert said, coming into my room to tell me.

'I shan't even try. And as it's mid-morning, can I offer you a cup of coffee from my machine? It's far better than that Arctic mud they provide for you in the clerk's room.'

'Last night I went out with Claude.'

'Who, you think, is a splendid character.'

'About whom I do now have certain feelings. Yes.'

'Has Claude told Phillida that he went out with you?'

'I don't think so. He needs help, Rumpole. I need to help him to restore his self-esteem.'

I thought that Claude's self-esteem was probably indestructible, but I refrained from saying so.

'Anyway, his wife, Phillida, said she was going to a conference of senior judges, very boring. Of course, the children were well able to look after themselves.'

'So what happened?'

'I wanted to see the new *Pirates of the Caribbean* movie and take a look at gorgeous Johnny Depp. Who do you think we saw in the queue ahead of us at the cinema in Leicester Square?'

'I've no idea.'

'Only Phillida and Mr Justice Bullingham. That's all!'

'Did they see you?'

'I don't think so. But she lied to him, Rumpole.

She never told him she was going out with a High Court judge.'

'And did Claude tell her he was going out with a single barrister?'

'No. But *I* didn't lie to Claude. I just went out.'

26

The warmth of early June had gone, to be followed by an uncertain summer with bright days, then high winds and pouring rain. The list of new judges came out and, in spite of his intervention in the Rumpole ASBO case and Leonard Bullingham's promise of support, Ballard's name was not among those picked.

'Uneasy is the head that relies on princes' favours,' I told Sam.

'I don't think Leonard Bullingham is a prince,' he answered. 'In fact he gained his scarlet and ermine by cosying up to the Lord Chancellor. I don't agree with that sort of thing. It's beneath contempt.'

I totally agreed. And I was not delighted to discover that on the list was the gloomy Barnes, the man with the looks of a discontented camel. It was this Barnes, you will remember, who had suggested that Rumpole spent his life trying to extricate the guilty from lawful punishment for their crimes.

It was therefore with some sinking of the heart that I learned the new judge was to be started off with a turn at the Old Bailey, where he was to try the tricky matter of the Queen against Graham Wetherby on the serious charge of murder.

'You still haven't got it, have you?' It was the first question my client asked me in the cell.

'Got what exactly?'

'The QC, of course.'

'No. But, as I told you, the committee have recommended me and the final decision has to come from the Minister, Peter Plaistow.'

'So I won't have a QC for the trial?'

'You may not have a QC but you'll have Rumpole of the Bailey. Stop worrying and let's just go quickly through the evidence again.'

27

'There can be few cases tried in this court, members of the jury, in which the facts point so clearly and inescapably to the guilt of the accused. We have no doubt at all that when you have heard the full story, whatever ingenious arguments my learned friend Mr Rumpole may put forward, this case can only have one conclusion, the conviction of Graham Wetherby on a charge of wilful murder.'

The speaker was Humphrey Noakes, QC, leading for the prosecution. He was a star of the Bar Golf Club. He wasn't the greatest lawyer in the world but the jury was being made to feel that he and they were normal people, as opposed to the devious Rumpole and his savage client.

Anna McKinnan was the first, and the most dangerous, witness for the prosecution. To remind you of her evidence, she testified that Wetherby arrived at the flat in Flyte Street shortly before one o'clock. After he'd paid her £110 she told him that the young lady wasn't with anyone else and he could go into the small sitting room and wait for her. If she didn't appear in a reasonable time he should knock on the bedroom door and she would call for him to come in. About twenty minutes later she heard Wetherby call out. She went in and found him standing by the bed. Ludmilla was lying across the bed, and she could see red marks around her neck.

Wetherby said nothing, so she locked the sitting-room door, which made him a prisoner, until the police arrived an hour later. He was then arrested and a police doctor examined Ludmilla's body.

Noakes ended by asking the witness to describe Ludmilla's character.

'I know people don't approve of what she did for a living, but she was a sweet girl, always cheerful and always kind to me. She never deserved what he did to her.'

This produced looks of sympathy and concern from the jury, so I knew that when I got up to cross-examine her I would be about as popular as a drunk interrupting a church service with an obscene joke. All the same, I had to challenge the witness.

'Miss McKinnan,' I tried to start in a friendly fashion, 'you have suggested that my client strangled Ludmilla.'

'I know he did.'

'And, having strangled her, he called you in to see what he had done.'

'He called out to me. Yes.'

'When what he could have done was to walk out of the flat and get clear away before you had discovered the body. Isn't that what you'd have done if you'd committed a murder?'

'Mr Rumpole!' Mr Justice Barnes interrupted for the first, but certainly not the last, time. 'This witness can't be asked what she would do if she had committed a murder. Her evidence is confined to what she saw.'

'And what she saw was apparently a murderer

who called attention to his crime and stayed to get arrested.'

'That is a comment you may make at the appropriate time. At the moment would you confine yourself to dealing with this lady's evidence!'

'Very well, My Lord.' I used the retort courteous, not wishing the jury to find me a difficult customer.

And then I asked her, 'Had you ever seen my client, Graham Wetherby, before that fatal afternoon?'

'Never at all. But I saw enough of him then.'

'So you had no reason to think he'd had any sort of quarrel with Ludmilla?'

'No.'

'Thank you for telling us that. So, within five minutes of meeting a total stranger, he decided to strangle her?'

'Sadly, our legal history is full, members of the jury,' Barnes decided to tell them, 'of murderers who have killed prostitutes without any apparent reason. It might be done from some perverted idea of ridding the world of such women.'

'You may choose to disregard His Lordship's reference to Jack the Ripper,' I told the jury. 'I'm afraid we have here a case of premature adjudication.' It was a telling phrase that I had used a few times before, and I was pleased to see that it raised smiles from at least three members of the jury.

'Manual strangulation might be a perverted part of the sex act, members of the jury,' Barnes suggested.

'He'd hardly been in her room for more than a minute or two,' I reasoned. 'Not enough time to get his trousers off, let alone have a fatal spasm of lust.'

This succeeded in silencing Barnes for a short while. So I turned my attention back to the witness.

'Let me ask you about Ludmilla. Did you know that she was imported from Russia in a crate on the back of a lorry?'

'I think she tried to tell me something like that. She couldn't speak much English.'

'Was she brought to your address in a people carrier from somewhere near Canary Wharf?'

'I don't know anything about that.'

'There, Mr Rumpole,' Barnes said with some pleasure, 'you've had your answer.'

'But you know there is an organization bringing in prostitutes from abroad, and Ludmilla was one of them?'

'I knew nothing about that.'

'Once again you have your answer,' the demented camel on the bench interrupted.

I gave the jury what I hoped was a look of hopeless resignation at an impossible judge, and then I got on to what I had decided was the most important part of the evidence.

'Do you remember a journalist called Lars Bergman?'

'I don't know that name.' It was the first time the witness had handed me an opening.

'But you remember a journalist coming to your address? He wanted Ludmilla to tell him the story of how she got to England, and her relationship with the group that brought her here.'

The witness had to agree reluctantly that she did remember the journalist.

'He might have said something like that.'

'Did Ludmilla agree to cooperate with him?'

'He said she had. He'd offered her a lot of money for her story.'

'I'm sure he did. But the organization didn't want the story told, did they?'

'Mr Rumpole,' Barnes weighed in again. 'I wonder what exactly this organization is?'

'Then wonder on, My Lord, till truth make all

things plain.' I did my best to silence him with a quotation, then turned back to the witness. 'The organization that brought Ludmilla here didn't want their story told, did they? And very soon afterwards her throat was wrung, so she could tell no more tales!'

'Mr Rumpole, who are you suggesting did this terrible deed?'

'Someone, My Lord, who had a far better motive for killing her than my unfortunate client. Someone who was afraid she'd tell the whole story. Someone killed her and made sure that her death would be blamed on the next available client. You knew that, Miss McKinnan, didn't you?'

There was a silence then. The witness, a middle-aged woman who might have been a hospital nurse, was looking round the court as if in the hope of finding some reasonable way of escape. She needn't have bothered. Barnes, of course, came to her rescue.

'It is my duty to remind you that you are not bound to answer any question which might incriminate you. Do you wish to answer Mr Rumpole's question?'

'It's an impertinence!' the witness said with obvious relief.

'I'm sure we would all agree with that,' Barnes couldn't resist saying. 'Do you intend to answer?'

'Certainly not.'

'There, Mr Rumpole.' Barnes gave me a mirthless smile. 'You've done your best!'

'My best, or my worst? I'll let the jury decide. I have no more questions.'

So I sat down, not altogether displeased with my cross-examination.

'That woman was lying!' That was my client's comment when I met him in the cells at lunchtime.

'Not at all. I made her tell the truth. It was very helpful.'

'And that judge! He's got no respect for you, Mr Rumpole.'

'The feeling is entirely mutual,' I assured him.

'Maybe he'll respect you a bit more when the QC comes through.'

'I don't expect so.'

'Why not?'

'I'm afraid the judge is out for a conviction. I'll have to disappoint him.'

As I left the cell my client slapped his forehead and said, 'Before I forget, Mr Rumpole. Helsing.'

'What do you mean exactly?'

'You asked me if I remembered the name. It came to me after you'd gone. It was a small firm of estate agents. We used them for accommodation when I was with human resources at the Home Office.'

'Thank you for that.' I was genuinely grateful but I tried not to sound too over-optimistic, even though I was beginning to feel that we might be in the clear. But there was still a lot to do and I had yet to cross-examine the police doctor.

'Dr Plater, you first saw the body of Ludmilla Ravenskaya when you arrived at about two-thirty. What did you find?'

'That death had been due to manual strangulation.'

'I think we're all agreed about that. What else did you notice?'

The doctor was a middle-aged man with a high forehead and a nervous smile. 'I'm not quite sure what you're referring to.'

'Well, for instance, were there signs of rigor mortis?'

'I did notice some stiffening of the joints, yes.'

'*Some* stiffening? Are you telling us that the stiffening was quite far advanced?'

'I thought it was. But I'd been told the time of death was only an hour before. So I felt I'd been mistaken.'

'And what if you weren't mistaken?'

'I'm not quite sure what you mean . . .'

'Neither am I, Mr Rumpole. You could put it more clearly to the doctor.' Mr Justice Barnes added his pennyworth.

'I mean that would have meant death two or three hours before your examination of the body.'

'Put like that, I suppose it's possible.'

'Did you notice anything about the girl's eyes?'

'Did I notice what about the eyes?'

'Did you notice, for example, black spots in her eyes?'

'Someone had shut her eyes. I opened them.'

'And were there black spots?'

'Something like that. Yes,' the doctor admitted reluctantly.

'And that would indicate death some three hours previously?'

'That is usually so, yes.'

'All you saw of that girl's body would indicate a death much longer before your examination than one hour?'

'In the usual course of events, yes.'

'In the usual course of events,' I repeated his answer to the jury.

Barnes told me not to attempt to make a speech until later. I didn't think the jury welcomed this intervention.

'I wasn't asked to consider the time of death.' The doctor looked apologetic.

'Well, you've been asked to consider it here and you have been extremely helpful. Thank you.'

28

I have left out many of the details in Wetherby. Statements of the accused had been produced, all of which protested his innocence.

The next day brought us Detective Inspector Belfrage, a large, avuncular figure. My job was to get him to be as helpful as possible without launching an all-out attack. A cosy chat between old friends was what I was aiming for.

'So, Detective Inspector Belfrage,' I started off, 'you have a long experience of cases of this sort, isn't that so?'

'I certainly have. And you've knocked around the criminal courts for a fairly long stretch as well.'

This brought a titter from the jury box, which was immediately silenced by the intervention of the gloomy Barnes.

'Mr Rumpole,' he said, 'this is a very serious case, so please make sure it proceeds in a serious manner.'

'Of course, My Lord. Nothing could be more serious than the wrongful conviction of an innocent man.' Then I turned to the inspector. 'I imagine you have traced the course of Ludmilla's life from the time of her arrival in England to her death in Flyte Street? You know that she was imported from Russia in a crate on the back of a lorry, like a consignment of chutney? And that when she was discovered at Dover she was allowed to stay here provided she reported to the police? Do you think it might be said that Home Office officials were being particularly lenient in her case?'

'Mr Rumpole, how can the officer possibly answer that?' Barnes had adopted his usual look of disapproval.

'Very well, My Lord. But would you agree, Inspector, that there are various criminal organizations dealing with the importation of foreign girls to be sent to work as prostitutes?'

'There are indeed. Young girls who have paid good money to be smuggled into England, where they have been promised good jobs and tempting wages. Once here they are forced into prostitution. That is happening, yes.'

'So let us look at this case. A Home Office official allowed her in. She's then taken to a building in the Canary Wharf area of London, where I shall prove that girls of her sort are temporarily confined. The ownership of the building has been traced to Helsing, a firm of estate agents occasionally used by the Home Office. From here she's put to work as a prostitute in Flyte Street. Does not all of that suggest that a serious and efficient organization was at work?'

'It certainly would seem so,' the inspector agreed.

'An organization of people who know their business?'

'I would say so, yes.'

'Perhaps an organization with connections to the Home Office itself?'

'Mr Rumpole! That's an outrageous suggestion!' The camel-like judge threw back his head and snorted with anger.

'This is an outrageous crime, My Lord.'

'I shall warn the jury to disregard anything you've said about the Home Office.'

'And I'm sure that the members of the jury will consider your advice very carefully before they decide whether or not to act upon it.' I paused then, before going on to my final question.

'If Ludmilla was about to tell her story to a journalist, the organization controlling her would have done everything in their power to stop this happening, wouldn't they?'

'I expect they would.'

'They might even not have stopped short of murder?'

There was what seemed like an endless pause while the inspector considered an answer which might win or lose the case.

'I suppose that is a possibility, yes.'

'Thank you, Inspector.' I sat down with a great sigh of relief. 'You've been extremely helpful.'

29

'Do you find it difficult to get girls to sleep with you?'

'With this on my face, what do you think?'

Graham Wetherby touched his spreading birth-mark and I hoped the jury understood. They sat stolidly and gave nothing away.

'Is that why you had to resort to sex with girls like Ludmilla Ravenskaya?'

'Yes, and I've usually found them very kind and understanding.'

'Is that how you expected to find Ludmilla?'

'Yes, but instead of that I found her dead.'

'And what did you feel when you found her dead?'

'Terribly sorry for her and angry with whoever did it.'

It wasn't a bad answer. Wetherby had proved to be an excellent witness. Even Noakes's earlier cross-examination, which seemed to go on forever, hadn't shaken him.

Was that because he was innocent, or because he was too good a liar? That was the question the jury would have to ask themselves.

When Wetherby left the box I started to enliven the proceedings by calling Fig Newton, who gave evidence about the premises near Canary Wharf.

'How is all this relevant to the present case, Mr Rumpole?' asked the judge. 'You're not suggesting that this witness saw Ludmilla at any point?'

'No, My Lord. An essential part of my case is that there was an efficient organization dealing in these unfortunate imported girls. This organization killed Ludmilla when they thought that she was about to tell her story to the press. Is Your Lordship suggesting that the jury should be denied this evidence?'

'I certainly am suggesting that, Mr Rumpole, and I'm looking at the clock. I shall rise now and come back into court at two o'clock, members of the jury.'

'Would Your Lordship say half past two? That'll give me time to get up to Fleet Street and make an application to the Court of Appeal.'

I saw a look of apprehension, even fear, flit across the camel's features, as though he felt he was about to step into some nasty hole in the desert sand.

'I will give a considered judgement on this matter at two o'clock. Perhaps you will delay your application to the Court of Appeal until you have heard what I have got to say.'

'If Your Lordship pleases.'

I gave the poor lost camel an encouraging pat and retired to the Old Bailey canteen to consume sausage, egg and chips with Bonny Bernard.

'I think we're on a winner,' I told him. 'A newly appointed judge doesn't want to have his decisions pissed upon by the Appeal Court.'

My forecast was right. The learned camel returned from his lunch with the judges and, with a sigh of resignation, said, 'You may call your evidence, Mr Rumpole, but keep it short.'

So, happily, the jury heard of girls imprisoned in the Canary Wharf building and then being driven round London and handed out like bottles of milk to customers. I even managed to get in the story of Mrs Englefield, who had now been questioned by the police.

When it was time for the final speeches, Noakes took the jury back through the evidence and then I got slowly to my feet.

After half an hour of commentary on all the facts, including the unanswerable question of why Graham Wetherby should have stayed there if he had committed the crime, I reached my peroration.

'*Possible*, members of the jury. I want you to have that word in your mind through all your deliberations. You have heard of the organization that ruthlessly controlled the lives of these girls. Is it not *possible* that when they thought Ludmilla was going to reveal their secret, they decided to silence her forever? You can't convict Wetherby unless you find him guilty beyond reasonable doubt. Once you find that another explanation of these events is *possible*, then you are left in a state of doubt. Above all things, remember what the police inspector in charge of this case said. It's a *possibility*, Detective Inspector Belfrage told us, that it was not Wetherby but this secret and illegal organization that put an end to the unhappy but young life of Ludmilla Ravenskaya. If you agree with this police officer, then you must be left in some doubt. It will then be your duty, and I trust it will be your pleasure, to acquit this young man of a horrible crime.'

So I sat down, hoping that I was leaving Barnes with no alternative but to agree to my definition of reasonable doubt.

He gathered up his papers and spent an hour and a half trying to avoid my irresistible conclusion, but in the end he failed. I hoped and thought that he still had an eye on the Court of Appeal.

Waiting for a jury to come back is always the worst time at the Old Bailey. There is nothing you can do other than consume too many cups of coffee and listen once again to Bonny Bernard's riveting account of his daughter's success in the inter-school netball semi-finals. This account was thankfully interrupted by a visit from our clerk, Henry, who'd come specially down to the Old Bailey with what he called 'an important spot of news'.

'It's about your application for QC, Mr Rumpole,' he said.

'They're about to wrap me in silk, are they?'

'I'm afraid not, Mr Rumpole. The Minister for Constitutional Affairs, he gets called the Minister of Justice now, has turned down your application.'

'Peter Plaistow, QC?'

'That's the one. They're saying around the Temple that you shouldn't have asked those questions about the Home Office.'

Further conversation on this matter was interrupted by the tannoy in the canteen announcing that the jury were going back to Court Number One.

As they came in, the members of the jury were looking at Wetherby in the dock. If they had failed to meet his eyes it would have been a sure sign of a conviction, but in ten minutes the case which had worried me, and I had lived with, for so long was over and Wetherby was a free man.

When I said goodbye, I told him, 'You see, it didn't make any difference my not getting a silk gown.'

'I'm sorry.' Wetherby looked more saddened by this than at any other time during the trial.

'Never mind,' I said. 'I can still be the oldest junior barrister around the Temple and I can win cases alone and without a leader.'

I suppose the words were brave, but I have to say that at that moment I found them entirely unconvincing.

30

What is there left to tell? The *Fortress* ran a story about the alleged involvement of a group within the Home Office in importing girls for prostitution. The Prime Minister told Parliament that this was an outrageous suggestion and he had every faith in the integrity of all civil servants.

Walking back to the Temple from the Law Courts one afternoon, I was caught up by Mrs Justice Erskine-Brown, who told me that she had just spent a weekend at a conference on sentencing at a country house near Winchester. 'It was all tremendous fun,' she said, 'and I have to tell you, Rumpole, that Leonard Bullingham has the most irresistible thighs.' Not wishing to hear any more about Mr Justice Bullingham's thighs, or indeed any other part of him, I turned off abruptly and sought sanctuary in Equity Court.

Scottie Thompson's friend Fred Atkins was at last apprehended by the police and in his statement after caution he admitted that he had never told Scottie about his human cargo. The case against Scottie was dropped after this rare example of honour among thieves.

One evening in Froxbury Mansions we were discussing young Peter Timson's ASBO case. I told Hilda that I had managed to get all the evidence in by telling the magistrate that the then Minister for Constitutional Affairs, Peter Plaistow, had said that witnesses in breach of ASBO cases should be cross-examined.

'And was that true?' Hilda asked me.

'Well, not exactly,' I had to admit, 'but that's what he ought to have said.'

Hilda shook her head sadly. 'Your profession has no sense of morality, Rumpole.'

'It was morally right that young Peter was acquitted.'

'I've come to a decision, Rumpole. After the way that you and Leonard have behaved, I'm going to give up my idea of reading for the Bar. I'm going down to Cornwall instead, where Dodo Mackintosh says we could have a great deal of fun sketching.'

So now I am back at my desk in Chambers, consuming an illegal sandwich and quaffing an illegal glass of wine. The life of an Old Bailey hack, I think to myself, has more ups and downs in it than the roller-coaster on the end of Brighton Pier. This is where it will all begin again.

Rumpole and the Reign of Terror

Rumpole is asked to defend a Pakistani doctor who has been imprisoned without charge or trial on suspicion of aiding Al Qaeda. Meanwhile, on the home front, She Who Must Be Obeyed is threatening to share her intimate view of her husband in a tell-all memoir. The result is Rumpole at his most ironic and indomitable, and John Mortimer at his most entertaining.

ISBN 978-0-14-311258-7

Rumpole and the Penge Bungalow Murders

John Mortimer tells the story of Rumpole's first and most formative case. Looking back half a century into a very different world, Rumpole recalls trying a case of patricide involving a pistol taken off a dead German flying officer. It was this trial and its outcome that shaped Rumpole into the lovable, exasperating, imposing figure readers know and love.

ISBN 978-0-14-303611-1

Rumpole and the Primrose Path

In these six stories, Horace Rumpole, despite having had a heart attack that left him at death's door in the previous volume, deftly parries everything from the admonitions of his wife, Hilda, to the vagaries of his legal colleagues and their new director of marketing, Luci—hired to give their chambers a slick new appearance. The title story finds him in a very dubious convalescent home battling a thin-lipped head nurse and befriending a junior one. Presuming Rumpole is soon to expire, Luci has been planning his memorial service, but the witty and irreverent Rumpole is far from hanging up his wig!

ISBN 978-0-14-200486-9

Rumpole Rests His Case
John Mortimer gives us seven fresh and funny stories in which the "great defender of muddled and sinful humanity" triumphs over the forces of prejudice and mean-mindedness while he tiptoes through the domestic territory of his imposing wife. With his passion for poetry, and a nose equally sensitive to the whiff of wrongdoing as to the bouquet of a Château Thames Embankment, the lovable and disheveled Rumpole "is at his rumpled best" (*The New York Times*).

ISBN 978-0-14-200347-3

The First Rumpole Omnibus
Includes *Rumpole of the Bailey, The Trials of Rumpole*, and *Rumpole's Return*.   ISBN 978-0-14-006768-2

The Second Rumpole Omnibus
Includes *Rumpole for the Defence, Rumpole and the Golden Thread*, and *Rumpole's Last Case*. ISBN 978-0-14-008958-5

The Third Rumpole Omnibus
Nineteen tales from *Rumpole and the Age of Miracles, Rumpole à la Carte*, and *Rumpole and the Angel of Death*.

ISBN 978-0-14-025741-0